Fragments

short stories and poems
by
Quirky Quills

Fragments

ISBN: 978-1-4716-9995-5

Fragments

sold in aid of

Ashgate Hospice

Ashgate Hospice is an independent registered charity that provides specialist palliative care (care to relieve pain rather than cure), both in the Hospice and community settings, for adults in North Derbyshire, High Peak and Dales. The needs of the patients, their families, friends and carers are fundamental to the philosophy of the Hospice.

Our aim is to enable people with palliative care requirements to have access to appropriate professional assistance and care and to help patients achieve the best possible quality of life in accordance with their wishes. We do not charge patients for the services we provide.

Ashgate Hospice has a full range of services provided by a multi-disciplinary team led by two Consultants in Palliative Medicine and includes Doctors, Nurses, Physiotherapists, Occupational Therapists, Social Workers, Lymphoedema team, Hospital-Based Nurses, Home Care, Bereavement Service and Chaplains. The Clinical team work together with a Support team of Caterers, Stewards, Housekeepers, Drivers, Groundsmen, Administrative, Finance and Fundraising staff to provide the excellent, specialised service that we are renowned for. Ashgate Hospice also provides education and training, support and advice in palliative care to health workers in the community.

Each year Ashgate Hospice provides care for around 3,000 adults with a terminal illness. Over 12,000 people are touched by the work of the hospice and at least 40 friends and family will be touched by the care we give each patient. No charge is ever made to any of our patients for the care they receive.

In order for us to continue providing the vital care outlined above we need to raise almost £3 million this year through voluntary giving.

Ashgate Hospice would like to express sincere thanks to the Quirky Quills for their very generous and kind support, Thank you!

Contents

for all those
who never knew they could do something
until they tried

Tuesday's Child

Run and hide, it's washday
The house is full of steam
And the smell of yellow soap
Clings halfway up the stairs
Grey ash floats on the kitchen air
From an infernal fire
Beneath the witch's cauldron
Boiling out guilty stains from bordered cloths
Beaten down with bleached wood cudgels
The grinding of greasy cogs
Labouring with each turn of a captive wheel
Handled by the skill of bloated hands
Tortures the innocent white twill
Between a rack of cruel rollers
Pouring back the poison blue water
Into a ribbed zinc tub,
Mated to its peg legged dolly
Stretching paddling pools along the terracotta floor
The fire has died
Frayed matting laid to rest
But the worst must still be borne
Run back and hide again
For an unnamed horse steals the comfort
From the heart warm range
Branding door stop irons to smoothing heat
Or match the scorched triangles
On a thrice fold blanket

Is it safe to come out of hiding?
To breathe the imprisoned blend
Of hot wet wool and yesterday's stew
Climb the wall to next door's yard
And so escape the sentence
Of the final airing
Till another week and another laden basket
Is saved up for a rainy day.

Jo M. Hudman

7

Chutney

When we moved into our new house we inherited a cat, called Glossop and a gardener called Chutney. We knew that we had inherited him because we had been told that he came with the garden. We didn't see him for a fortnight. Suddenly one morning he was there, working in the garden. We had been assured that he was a real treasure, and that we were very lucky to have him.

Our new house was in the village of Fording Hough. It was built about 1880 in the Arts and Crafts style with brick, a tiled roof and oak timberwork throughout. We were quite excited to find it.

Our family consists of me, Joyce Plumpton, my husband Desmond and our two children Olive 14 and Richard 12. We had moved from a town having decided that we would have a better life in a village. Fording Hough has two pubs, The Knightly Arms and The Kings Head; a post office and a general store. The village hall, built to celebrate Queen Victoria's Diamond Jubilee, is where all the village activities take place. The Library van visits once a week and there is a travelling butcher who seems to turn up on a Wednesday or Thursday depending on some event that I have not fathomed.

Sadly the village school closed in the sixties and all the children are bussed off at eight-thirty in the morning to the big school in town.

Desmond is a research Chemist and works for Briden Chemicals. They do general business based upon coal tar products. I used to work there but left when we got married.

When I saw Chutney in the garden one morning I went out to introduce myself. He was concentrating on digging a vegetable bed and I could hear him singing a hymn to himself. I coughed discreetly as I approached.

"Good morning Chutney," I called.

"Morning Mistress," he replied.

"My name is Joyce," I said. "What time would you like coffee?"

"Thank you Mistress but I always brings my flask." There was a pause. "I always takes my breaks in my shed."

I got used to being told that I was his mistress, but he called all the ladies that he worked for 'mistress'.

I remember that when we had a look round the house and garden, the shed had been pointed out to us as being the sole property of the gardener. It seemed odd at the time; we accepted it as a country way and did not question it.

Our garden is very spacious. It runs to about two acres. It was one of the things that attracted us to it. It comprises a long wide front with a drive with in and out as access to the road. At the back of the property there is a long lawn interspersed with flower beds. The overall effect is rather pleasant. We get long lawn vistas and as we walk up the garden it opens to new pathways and views over the rolling Buckinghamshire countryside. In the far corner away from the rest of the garden is a small enclosed plot about the size of the garden that we had at our town house. Within this plot is the substantial shed that belongs to Chutney. We discovered later that he has three sheds on three plots in the gardens that he maintains in the village.

Chutney looks about fifty but some say that he is in his seventies. Everyone that you speak to tells you that he was born in the village but no one can remember his parents. He lives rent free in a cottage that is owned by the Knightly family who once lived in the manor house that is defunct and long gone. I was told in confidence that he was the bastard son of the old squire who left a legacy for his continued survival. I was also told, again in the strictest confidence, that his father had saved one of the Knightly sons in the First World War; or it could have been the Boar War depending who you listen to. Most folk agree that he has some unspecified connection to the Knightly family.

It is evident to look at him, that he was once a handsome man. His face is now tanned and under a white thatch of hair are bright sparkling blue eyes. He always seems to wear moleskin trousers, ex army braces and bright colourful shirts. His feet are for ever shod in army boots. He has an encyclopaedic knowledge of the countryside and of gardening which he shares with anyone who cares to ask. Many do. His closest companion is a hen Raven called Blackie that he raised from a fledgling. Each year she would be courted and then raise a family in the high Black poplar tree. When the youngsters are fledged she returns to Chutney and they winter together.

Somehow marriage seemed to have passed him by. His washing is done by Widow Jenkins at one end of the village and he often eats at the other end of the village with Widow Gore-Smith.

I took the children to meet Chutney after they were settled and had sorted out their rooms. When they saw the Raven and the way in which she seemed to guard her companion they were spellbound by her. Soon the children were seeking out Chutney for his fund of countryside stories. Soon it was, 'Chutney says this or that.' Children of their age are much more direct. They would pose personal questions that I would never dare ask. It was from them that I learnt that he often slept during the summer months in one or other of his huts. When he wanted tools for the garden he would go to a solicitor in the village and he would provide them free of charge. He always uses his own tools, never anybody else's. It was rumoured that he was a very rich man; having a modest income for which he had little need. I always paid him cash. He had no bank account apparently, although from the children I learnt that the Solicitor acts as his banker. When he has too much cash the Solicitor gets a seed packet stuffed with bank notes pushed through his front door.

In winter when there is little work he retires back to the cottage and has a log fire that keeps both Blackie and him very snug. Sunday is a day of rest for Chutney He attends St Stephen's Church in his best suit morning and evening and enjoys the hymns. He has never owned a radio or television. The children asked him if he had ever been to see a film at the cinema. He admitted that many years ago he went with his younger brother and saw a film about some gangsters in America. He said that there was too much killing and never went again. On Saturday evening he attends the Knightly Arms and has just one pint that he gets in exchange for some garden produce.

I was intrigued to know why he was called Chutney, and so I

prompted the children to ask him. He told them that it was just something that he was called and that he could not remember his real name any more. I was sure that there was more to it than that, and so I asked around. Nobody knew. It was something that he had always been called.

I could not fault him in the garden. The fruit trees were bountiful due to his attention as were the vegetable plots. The lawns were weed free and always cut to perfection and verdant. I would get a regular supply of garden produce and cut flowers for the house. If I went into the garden while he was there I would hear him singing his hymns and see Blackie guarding him from a high vantage point or else sitting on his shoulder.

Then suddenly Chutney died. He was in his shed in our garden. We knew something was wrong because Blackie was hopping around very upset. People say that birds are just silly, but Blackie kept pecking on my kitchen window until I went outside. She drew me to the Chutney's shed where I found him in his daybed, gone from this world into the next.

The church was very full when we attended the funeral of our dear friend. But the biggest surprise was when the vicar named him as out dear departed brother, the right honourable Sir Chisholm Knightly known to his many friends as Chutney.

We have a new gardener now and we have adopted a Raven called Blackie. Although somehow I think that it is truer to say she adopted us.

Clive Holliday

Autumn

Rustic leaves swirl underfoot as I run across the park, chasing a dream. Daylight fades. He stands, waiting, a dog sitting by his legs.

Tears well as I slow down; street lights blaze into life. I'm standing beneath a tree. Can I hide? Hide the tears that roll down my face? Memories float before me like autumn leaves: some dark, others golden.

Startled by something scratching at my legs, I feel cold sweat on my body. Unable to move, a mumbled cry leaves my lips. "Go away, get down! Why can't I wake? Please let me wake up, there's something on my bed. Go away!"

I manage to sit up. Still in a daze, I jump out of bed. My heart is palpitating as I reach out to switch on the light. Nothing there – on the bed or in the covers – but it felt so real.

Opening the bedroom door, I find my way to the kitchen, though not before I walk into the coffee table of the unfamiliar apartment in Spain. I mustn't grumble, it was a free holiday gift from a friend. Finally I find the cups and click the kettle on, trying not to wake Sally in the other room, and I'm thankful for the bright street lighting.

Sally walks into the room, blonde hair looking like a frightened Busby.

"What are you doing, Jemmy? It's 3am."

She slumps down in a chair. Her crumpled burgundy dressing gown promotes an image of leaves which have fallen from a bush. She shifts position, her white feet and toes complete with red and green nail varnish are languidly resting over the chair edge, looking like holly berries.

"Here you are, this will warm you." She takes the hot drink and I sit in the opposite chair and turn on the standard lamp. "I love the autumn air, it's always so fresh and new even in the midst of death."

"What are you prattling on about, Jemmy? Did you put some Sheridan's in your coffee?"

"No, silly. I have just had the weirdest night. . . . A dog curled up on my legs while I slept and it wouldn't get down."

"It won't, in your dreams. You should have tossed it a bone!" Sally is trying to make light of her friend's experience, knowing only too well how sensitive she is.

A tree branch taps the window. Jemmy jumps, then shivers and goes to switch on the fire. "That's better. Look, its raining, Sally."

"Yeah, I hope it clears up by tomorrow, Ritchie is coming to take us out and he wants to show us that cove at Pontyiano."

"Not before we crunch seeds under foot. This rain will fetch them down. Autumn has such a tenuous hold on life."

"Yeah, yeah, Jemmy, you and your poetry. You know autumn can be damned dirty. It's not nice when the juice of those berries squelches all over my shoes. You can't get it off you know, it's like a permanent dye." Sally stifles a yawn. "I'm off to finish my beauty sleep. See you in three hours. Night, Jemmy."

"G'night, Sally. Wait... here, your curler dropped out of your fringe."
They both laugh.

Jemmy begins to fall asleep in the recliner chair wrapped in the white duvet Sally has thrown over to her. She snuggles down and slips into sleep.

Early morning finds both girls very bright considering their ruffled night. Jemmy has cooked vegetarian brunch for breakfast. Sally helped, giggling as she put the food on two plates. No tureens or fancy dishes here, they knew what each other liked.

"Well, Sally, that is truly autumnal." Then she bows; the mushrooms edged around an egg, with sliced, fake sausages for a mouth, splashes of tomatoes as rosy cheeks and all on a slice of toast.

"What time are we going to the cove? I want to take a walk first."

"You have lots of time, Jemmy. We're not leaving till ten o'clock."

They eat breakfast in silence. Afterwards Sally goes to her room. Jemmy leaves for her run, to return an hour later and went straight into the shower.

Just before ten o'clock, Sally calls to her friend: "Are you ready, Jemmy? Ritchie will be here soon."

"Can you go on your own, Sally? I'm going out for lunch to Vega-a – One."

"Oh, and who are you meeting?"

"Well, in the dream I had last night I saw a man with a dog in the park watching me. I know it has been a couple of years now. . . I thought, maybe it was my late husband, telling me he was looking after our dog that passed away. Now it seems I was wrong. I met Neil and his dog Cha-chi in the park. Neil invited me to lunch."

"Get you! Autumn seems to be your season. Little seeds deep in leafy compost sit. Have a good time; I'll see you this evening... if you are back."

*****

The next few days would bring excitement for both of them. Sally because Ritchie would show her all the sights and Jemmy with her Neil. Although, Jemmy, being Jemmy, would insist on going dutch for their evening dates. However, she would also allow him to buy her lunch and coffee on the days they walked his dog.

Eventually, the girls had to say farewell. This was done at the apartment. Then they got into their taxi to the airport, for the return home journey, both were in high spirits.

Jemmy goes to fetch Kejo, her mongrel from the boarding kennels. She is met by a very sedentary dog, not at all his usually fussy self.

"He's been pining," says Fiona, the kennel lady. "We thought we would have to phone you on Wednesday evening; he was ill and wouldn't settle."

Jemmy's astonished mind races; that was the evening she had felt something try to curl up on her bed. She scoops up Kejo. "Maybe we should change your name to Blue, instead of my two dead husbands Kevin and John"

Blue barks in agreement. He gives his mistress a paw as she straps him into the car, happy to go home.

Elizabeth Procter

Resolution

Despite all the horror, Millie loved her husband. She bore the wounds he inflicted, looked after the house, kept herself slim, hid bruises under make-up and strategically placed clothes, looked after him when he was ill, and apologised to the neighbours for "moving the furniture so late at night". Mrs Tate next door, fortunately, never questioned Millie's lies.

As the time between the wedding and the present elapsed, Max' anger swelled. Millie was unable to put reason to his actions, and the only action she was able to take was to succumb to it. Max' fury could be fuelled by his perception of interest in Millie by any other man. To that end, Millie's life became easier when she left her job, thus minimising her contact with other people and quenching Max' thirsty anger, temporarily at least.

When Millie stopped going to work Max was more amiable than at any other point in their marriage. When, one Sunday morning, Millie intended to pop out to the local shop for a pint of milk for their breakfasts, Max' temper rose in a characteristic blaze of fury, and as a result the pain and bruising he inflicted on her lasted longer than ever before. Millie resigned herself to accept that the less she left the house, the more difficult it was becoming for her to do so.

Millie's family and friends could tell something was wrong in her marriage. She became increasingly afraid, reluctant to invite them round, and stopped going out to visit them. Millie's love for her husband, despite his fierce anger, shielded them from the truth; that he inflicted physical and psychological torture upon her relentlessly. Her ex-workmates attempted to remain in contact with her, but soon tired of their fruitless efforts and left her to her own devices. Millie became increasingly introverted and resigned to her marriage, to the extent that she ceased begging Max not to hurt her, instead accepting his actions unquestioningly.

Millie busied herself with thoughts of the effect her husband's furious anger must have on his health. She imagined all the tiny raging synapses firing inside his brain, the messages sent to his body, and the actions he took. She minimised his anger by maintaining obsessively high levels of tidiness and cleanliness in the house, and by succumbing to his vicious needs silently. She was entirely resigned to her life, because, despite all the horror, she loved her husband.

It was a summer morning when Max, charming Mrs Tate over the fence on his way to work, collapsed. Millie, watching him leave from the doorway, ran to him, cradled his head in her lap, and soothed him while Mrs Tate phoned for an ambulance.

The hospital confirmed that Max had suffered a massive stroke. His physical functions were catastrophically affected but it was believed his cognitive functions were fully intact. Millie visited her husband whenever the hospital would allow it, even stayed overnight with Max at times. The staff whispered of her loyalty. They advised Millie that he would require twenty-four hour nursing care after leaving hospital. Millie promised them that she would provide all the care he needed at home.

Max went home three months after the stroke, having made a little physical progress, but still unable to communicate, and fully dependent for all his needs. This was the happiest time of Millie's life.

Millie provided thorough and loving care for Max. She fed him the liquidised organic meals she had made, assisted him with all his personal care requirements, talked to him openly about anything and everything, invited her family and friends to visit them both. She went out to meet friends and ex-workmates and Mrs Tate would sit with Max.

Millie's favourite part of the day was bed time. She would help Max into bed, ensure he was comfortable and talk to him about her day. Before turning the light out she would lean over to kiss him goodnight, and look into his eyes.

She could still see the fury raging there.

Millie would then lie close to her husband and drift off to sleep thinking about what a wonderful life she had, and how safe she felt.

Kate Singleton

The Eagle Has Landed

It all started after Dave's death. An amicable divorce five years ago resulted in our lovely daughter, Julie, living with me, Dave's new partner Fiona permanently residing with him. But then how permanent is *permanent* these days?

Julie would visit them most weekends; whenever they went on vacation, he would always send a text to the mobile phone he'd bought her for Christmas, and always the same phrase: 'The Eagle has landed , the place is just wonderful.' The idea came from the two of them watching the film of the same title, a Dave favourite. In fact anything he liked then so did our ten-year old daughter. They adored each other.

Busy with the accounts for my flower shop, a breathless Julie rushed into the office, a big smile on her face, and waving her phone. Didn't need more than one guess who the text was from: Dave and Fiona had flown to Lyon that morning for a week's break.

"Mummy, Mummy."

I smiled. "I know. 'The Eagle has landed'."

A week later my father passed away. I was getting ready to visit the Chapel of Rest when Julie came into my bedroom.

"Mummy, please can I come with you to see Granddad?"

"Oh darling, I don't think it's very appropriate for a ten-year old to see an old man in his coffin."

"Why not? Alison at school went to see her granddad when he died; she said he just looked as if he was asleep. Oh come on, Mum, I'm not a baby anymore! I would like to say goodbye to him."

We talked it over, me feeling unsure as to what effect it might have on her young life. In the end I gave in.

As it happened my reasons for concern were unfounded. On seeing my father in his coffin she wasn't at all perturbed, quite the opposite. She placed her hand over his ice-cold fingers, and then kissed his forehead. A teardrop landed on his lips as she pulled away.

That weekend we'd arranged for Julie, already over the moon about Fiona's pregnancy, to stay over at her dad's house. I'd already been informed she would be busy helping to get a new nursery ready, ideal to take her mind off her grandfather's passing.

On the Sunday evening Fiona brought Julie home.

"You coming in for a coffee, Fiona?"

"Not tonight thanks Bev, I've left Dave doing some wiring, I told him to get a qualified electrician in but… Well you know what he's like."

Julie clutched my hand as we climbed the steps to the front door; we turned and waved to Fiona as she drove away. All in a tizzy, Julie squeezed my hand.

"Ooh Mummy I'm so excited, just think in two months time I shall have a little brother to help look after."

"It might be a girl."

"No its not, they told Fiona at the hospital it was a boy. I've always wanted a brother, now I'm going to have one."

Later that same evening, just after Julie had gone to bed, I received a fretful phone call from Fiona's mother.

"Hello Bev, sorry to be the bearer of bad news but I'm afraid Dave has had an accident, he's been electrocuted. An ambulance has just collected him and taken him to the local hospital. As you can imagine the whole incident has all been too much for Fiona I thought it wise and sent for the doctor to come and see her. She is in a bad way. She's asked if you wouldn't mind going to the hospital for her."

With Julie to consider, her having school the following day, I didn't wake her. Thank goodness for good neighbours. Mrs Wilson next door sometimes looked after Julie if ever I had to work late at the shop.

"No problem, love. Just give me five minutes to finish our Grahams pack up, he's on night duty all this week."

Mrs Wilson was as good as her word. There wasn't a lot I could do. I went to see Dave and confess to a tear given the time we'd spent together. Goodbyes said, I stopped off to see how Fiona was. Her mother told me she was sleeping, exactly what I wanted to do. But oh heck, what a shock for Julie to face in the morning, first her granddad, now her beloved father. And another visit to the Chapel of Rest so soon after.

It would be about a month afterwards that I kept receiving unusual texts on my mobile. The first one said 'Feeling great . . . pain has gone.' The second one arrived a few days later: 'Thank you' it stated with a kiss. Another 'What beautiful flowers, most grateful.' This went on for some while. First I thought it must have been satisfied customers, but they usually came into the flower shop to say it in person, or via a thank you note, sometimes a letter, but never by mobile phone. The weird thing is, when I replied, the message was the same for each: 'Number not recognised'.

I met up with my friends for lunch as we did on a regular basis. I told them about the messages I'd received. Jenny thought I should go to the police; Liz suggested I throw away the phone and buy a new one. "Have you phoned back?" asked Ann. I told her the number was not available. Suppose I could have done as Liz suggested, but get a new sim card rather than dispose of the phone. Either way I was determined to have the whole sorry mess dealt with.

Reluctantly I decided to ask Julie if she'd received any unusual messages thinking perhaps it was a school kid having a joke. After dinner that evening, I laughingly told her, attempting to make light of it all, without wishing to worry her.

But I didn't laugh for long when she told me who the phone calls were from.

"Mummy, they're from Daddy!" She said it as if it were quite a natural phenomenon. I could feel my colour drain as the words left her mouth.

"You remember when we went to the chapel of rest?" she said. "Well I put his mobile phone under his shroud, with the words 'Text me." I got a message from him last Saturday saying 'The Eagle has landed, and the place is just wonderful.'

"Mummy you're crying. Did I do the wrong thing?"

Ann Hodgson

Three Gatekeepers

I should be *more kind* to those I interact with,
those artists and philosophers, writers and madmen
with whom I share the passing of days.

A woman wise beyond her years
introduced my to an Arabian proverb
"The words of the tongue should have three gatekeepers."
A philosophy I should strive to live by.

The first gatekeeper asks 'Is it true?'
which prevents my telling tales without verifying facts,
puts an end to gossip and speculation
and varnishes my soul with trust.

The second asks 'Is it kind?'
and while by law it may not be kind to speak of all I've seen,
in everyday the truths and spites and little white lies
with which we decorate our hermit shells
weigh us down but yet a smile can be teased
with such a simple thing.
"What lovely hair you have, my dear."

The keeper of the third is hardest of all to please –
she asks of all the words that come: "Is it necessary?'
And I confess that much is not but were there not a means
to ask this one to turn away and let some slip through
the world would be a duller place indeed,
with no time for talk and social niceties,
nor novelists!

For what are we but liars of the cruellest sort
who peddle words of men who never lived
and deeds not done at all and only dreamed.

But in the waking world I'll strive to honour two of these
and next year seek to censure thought as well
and keep my barbs and knives yet free of bloodied fools.

Rachel Green

Resolution

Alfred Jones shivered and wrapped his dressing gown more closely about him. It was not only the chill of the night that made him shiver.

It was 2-45a.m. in early June and Jones felt distinctly unlucky that he had been chosen for this undertaking. He stood in the gloom at the end of his bed in the middle of the dormitory, aware that seven pairs of eyes were silently watching.

They were all twelve years old and term boarders at the Harry Fenchurch public school, their fees paid by middle class parents who expected high achievement.

"Go on, Jones, get on with it," a voice eventually hissed from the darkness.

Jones slowly walked to the door at the end of the dormitory. The door led to the corridor, the stairs, another corridor and finally the music room below where they were taught music composition.

Jones nervously stepped out, leaving the door wide open behind him.

Earlier that day the music teacher, Mr. Simpson, had showed the class how important it was for music compositions to finish favourably, or to resolve. As he put it, "The listener has to be satisfied that the musical story has definitely come to a conclusion much as a story in a book, a play or a film. That feeling of satisfaction in the listener will promote the feeling of wanting more from that particular composer, thus fostering a growing fondness for great music."

The boys had listened, trying to understand what Mr Simpson was talking about. Although young, they instinctively recognized that he was not just a music teacher. He had a deeply felt love of all things musical.

In Mr. Simpson's mind, music was the international language, transcending politics, race and culture. It could be said that for Mr Simpson it had replaced religion. The boys could all see this from his facial expression and demeanour when discussing music.

The boys had a respect for Mr Simpson that was not shared with any other teacher.

When the boys had finished lessons for the day and were taking a break in their dormitory before studies, Collinson, the boy who had been studying piano since his fifth birthday, suddenly blurted out, "I know exactly what Simpson meant today." When the jibes of "Yeah, you would, wouldn't you, Rachmaninov…" and the ensuing laughter had died down, Collinson succeeded in educating the rest by singing a scale in such a way as to leave no doubt about what resolution really meant.

The idea of the joke was born out of the following fifteen minutes of amused, animated and occasionally hilarious chatter.

Mr. Simpson's rooms were up a short flight of stairs at the other end of the ground floor corridor, and were situated above the music room. The boys decided, with some glee, that this was ideal.

Jones, being the one who had picked the short straw, had made his way down to the bottom corridor and was slowly and silently opening the door to the music room, leaving it wide open not only for sound dispersal but for his quick escape! The moon projected crazy squares of light into the room from the ancient leaded windows. Heart beating loudly in his ears, he gently lifted the lid of the Steinway upright piano which was positioned across a corner at the front of the classroom. The white keys were easy to see in the gloom. Jones put out a shaking index finger above middle C.

He had been instructed by the others to say "one thousand" in his head between each note, which would give a gap of approximately one second. Taking a deep breath, he plunged his finger hard onto the key.

The loudness made him start. It seemed to split the night like an axe. Saying one thousand in his head, Jones struck the key again and again and yet a fourth time, saying one thousand in his head between each strike. They had all agreed Mr Simpson should be awake by now.

Jones now hit the D key (one thousand), E key (one thousand), F, G, A, and finally B. Jones closed the piano lid with both hands shaking and with trembling legs he fled along the corridor, up the stairs, along the top corridor and through the wide open door into the dormitory where he flung himself onto his bed, gasping.

"Brilliant," "Ace," "Nice one, Jones," "Criminal," were some of the whispered comments he heard as he lay there in the dark, panting.

A mere forty seconds had elapsed since Jones' last note. The dormitory fell silent. The boys listened intently. Collinson had agreed to keep time on the watch his parents had given him as a bribe when he had his first music lesson. It was a Smiths pocket watch with a luminous dial. Although large, in nineteen fifty two this was a prized timepiece.

*****

When the second note struck, Mr Simpson's deep slumber was already accelerating into awareness. With the third note, one eye was opened and after the fourth, his other eye. While his mind tried to piece together what was happening and was still prepared to accept it may be a dream, the D and E sounded. Mr Simpson's eyes widened. He was fully awake now.

He heard F, G, then A. Then B. Silence. He knew this was the B4 and should be followed by C5. But silence.

He tried singing in his head "do re mi fa so la ti do".

But Mr Simpson still heard the B. That note sounded louder than the others. Had it been louder? Did it still sound? He thought not. Yet that B still resonated inside his head like no other note had ever done. It lingered and lingered. Mr Simpson's whole mind and body shouted that the first note heard was C4. Yet the last note was B4. It was unfinished, unfinished! Where was C5?

One minute later, even as Mr Simpson pulled the bedclothes around his head in a desperate attempt to shut out the still sounding B, he knew that he had lost this battle. Sighing resignedly, he threw back the sheets and reached for his dressing gown.

Eight pairs of ears in the dormitory above heard the sound of the next C above middle C. The forgiveness of the C5. Loud but not too loud. But very, very firm. The last sounding B4 struck by Jones had at last been resolved up one semitone to C5.

"Two minutes fifty five seconds from the last note," announced Collinson.

Two days later, at the commencement of the music lesson, Mr Simpson stared intently at his class and, with a twinkle in his eye, said, " Well, boys, I am very pleased that my previous lesson about resolution was so fully understood by you all. Even I learnt a little from it, too!"

The boys smiled, knowing everyone in the room had enjoyed the joke and Mr Simpson earned even more respect that day.

Keith Singleton

Lost Village

Nestled in seclusion
Was the valley of the damned
Its people as hardy as the fir trees
Thick upon the sheltering hills
Where lofty crags stood guard from ancient times
Made verdant by the crumpled ribbon
of its stream unwinding out of distant hills

When demands of wasteful cities grew
Engineers were summoned
To weigh the balance against conservation pleas
But the scales tipped down on the side of necessity
Water not sentiment for an exploded population.

Soon the virtuous springs were refused
Their seasoning with the salt rich seas
Blocked by limestone weather worn
Torn from the wild unyielding heather
Cemented into cubic alphabets.

Then the priceless bounty seeped through every slit
Silted up the doorsteps
Lapped around the lintels of doors
Once opened to a warming welcome
Forced an entry into vacant bedrooms
To have its way on love lorn mattresses.

Drowned the sound of Post Office gossip
Blinded the eyelets of packhorse bridge
Pondering its inverted image
On sleepy afternoons
Silenced the pious steeple bell
Where irreverent minnows
Haunt the exhumed graves

Fortunate the sightless windows
Not to see the sad procession
Topped and tailed of roof and root
Signing the lease of raw new dwellings
Daring a backward glance
To mourn their ancesters' way
The day a village died.

Jo M. Hudman

<u>Lost</u>

Bo lived in a beautiful little house in Madeira, way up high in the mountains. It was a quaint house built in the shape of a capital A. Downstairs there was a lounge and a dining room and upstairs there was a bedroom. The house was too small to accommodate a kitchen so it was located in an outhouse. When Bo was twenty-one her parents decided to move to the bottom of the mountain where new bungalows had been built. They left the house to Bo as her twenty-first birthday gift.

Bo's life was quite self sufficient, keeping hens, sheep and goats. During the summer the animals could fend for themselves but winter months meant a lot more work. Her main concern was for the sheep and goats that had wandered too far up the mountain sides and it was important that, before the freezing fogs began, she brought them to lower ground where they would have more shelter from the harsh weather.

All this work was fine when Bo was younger but now her age was telling and it took her much longer to climb the mountains. It was okay when her fiancé was in her life, he would help with the farm and the animals' safety. Bo and Robert were so happy in the first few years but as time went on Robert became subdued. One day whilst having one of their picnics up on the mountain he poured his heart out to Bo. He told her that he needed more out of life and wanted to leave the village. So on that day on the mountain a six year old love was lost.

All that was ten years ago. Bo was now thirty-six years old. On his rounds Patrick, the postman, would bring her up to date with any news of Robert. He reported to Bo when Robert had gained his HNC certificate in the building trade and was now working for himself on the mainland of Portugal but was hoping to return to Madeira as soon as he had made enough money.

Rounding the corner in his little red van the post man made his weekly deliveries to the mountain folk who lived few and far between. It took Patrick the best part of a day just doing the mountain deliveries, but he loved it. He would always start at the top waving to all the neighbours on his way up. Little Charlene and Scott would stand on their doorstep looking out for the red van, then wave excitedly when Patrick passed. He would be invited into various homes like one of the family. One of his last calls was to Bo's house. Patrick had a lot of time for her, especially as she did not see many folks, living alone as she did.

"Hello, Patrick, do come in, I've made your special cake today."

"Thought I smelled something mouth-watering. I could smell it all the way down the hill. Well, you seem to have a lot of post today, my dear, hope its all good."

They sat and chatted as Patrick brought all the gossip from Funchal. Finishing his third cup of tea Pat stood to go.

"Any messages to the folk below then, Bo?"

"Ooh yes, here, I've made a list. Could you explain to Robert that I'm getting desperate for my chimney to be fixed before the bad weather comes?"

"I'll be sure to tell him. Let's face it, the nights are drawing in. Oh, how I do hate these foggy, misty days of October. Bye for now, see you next week."

It was exactly one week later when Robert followed the sweet aroma towards Bo's kitchen and there she was, surrounded by rising dough, fairy cakes and, most important of all a mixture of Madeira cake ready to go into the oven. Robert explained to her that he would come back later that day. Bo was so pleased that at last the chimney would be fixed. It had caused Bo sleepless nights, not knowing if the chimney stack would collapse on top of her in those awful winds. It was not long after Robert left her doorstep that Patrick arrived.

"One letter, one bill by the looks of it," he announced, placing the two envelopes on the kitchen table, then cheekily sat whilst Bo brought him refreshments. It was such an old routine by now that neither of them thought anything of it. Bo looked forward to Patrick's company on his weekly visits; she was so busy with her own chores it was quite rare for her to visit the village. Just as Patrick stood to take his leave Bo remembered something.

"Patrick, I'm sure you'll see Robert on your travels so will you tell him I may be out when he calls later?"

"Oh yes? You got a date then, Bo?" Patrick teased.

"No, it's just that I have a lame sheep that tends to get herself stuck up on the mountainside. The others are pretty good when I go to call them at dusk but I think this one gets herself too high up then panics when she can't turn around to come back down, so I have to go and find her and give her a helping hand."

"You want to be careful yourself, up there when the light's going, could be dangerous."

"Come on Patrick, you know me better than that. How many years have I been doing this and in all weathers? I'll be fine."

Patrick was not convinced by Bo's confidence. He just made a huffing sound and went through the kitchen door shaking his head, wishing he could do more for this sweet, hard working woman who struggled through life on her own.

Robert was just putting the finishing touches to the chimney stack rebuild when he heard a call from below.

"Down in a minute, didn't realise how dark it had got, I've been so busy focused on what's in front of me."

Robert came safely down and stood by Patrick, then looked up to admire his handy-work.

"If you can see that chimney you're looking for then you've better eye sight than me, Robert," Patrick was right. The mist was so bad by now he couldn't see the roof let alone the chimney.

"I came to ask Bo if I might stay the night on her couch, the weather's so bad I can't find my way home."

"Never realised the weather had changed so much, so intent on my handy-work I was! Well I never!" said Robert looking around him. "There's no way we can get down to the village tonight, let's hope Bo has two couches, eh?"

"Well, there goes another problem. Bo's not in and I'll tell you I'm worried about her. I think she's still up there with those dratted sheep."

Robert switched on the light on his hard hat facing the direction in which Bo's sheep collected themselves into their rightful pens and there they were, huddled together for warmth just as they should be. But where was Bo?

"It'll be that lame, black sheep. She's soft enough to go to find it, after all I said to her this morning."

Robert was about to start the climb up the mountain when through the mist Bo appeared. Within the hour they were all safely down and there they were, sipping hot chocolate around the kitchen fire; Bob the builder, Postman Pat, and Little Bo Peep clutching Baa Baa Black Sheep on her knee.

Ann Hodgson

All down to a butterfly

We were good friends. She was the sort of friend that you trust to take your child to school, that you lend your dress patterns to, that you bake a cake for when she's not feeling so good. The sort of friend you can ask to baby sit when your husband is working late and you have to visit your mother. That sort of friend.

We lived only four houses apart on a street where people minded their own business but would roll your wheelie bin out on a Friday morning if you'd forgotten. When I had Alice, my daughter, and Janet had her second son we met at all the local baby things; the ante-natal clinic, post natal clinic, baby weighing clinic and so on.

"Come back to my house, if you don't mind the mess," she said one morning after we both got full marks from the nurse at the health centre. "The babies can goo at each other and we'll have a coffee."

We chatted all the way home, each of us pushing a buggy laden with a small baby, a bag of groceries and a pack of nappies.

We laughed a lot, and I tackled the chores with a lighter step that afternoon. It became a habit. On a normal day we would sit in each other's kitchen and drink a couple of mugs of coffee. We talked through every topic you could imagine, from sewing an outfit for a child to planting lettuces, the cost of a tin of paint, how to stretch a pound of mince. Once the caffeine kicked in we could face the rest of the day.

Gradually we started to rely on each other. When Janet wanted to go to town I would mind little Jacob for her. If my mother needed me I would drop Alice off on my way to the bus stop.

Our friendship was exclusive of our family lives. Once our husbands were home a line was drawn and only in exceptional circumstances would we contact each other. Then, as the children started to grow up they became friends too. All too soon we were buying their school uniforms and packing lunch boxes.

We walked to school together that first morning, a little procession with her older boy shepherding the younger two safely along the route. I helped Alice hang her coat on her Elephant coat peg and settled her with a book, then left quickly with her new brother before she saw the tears in my eyes.

I pushed my baby son home and put on the kettle. I expected to hear Janet's knock, but she didn't come that morning so I took the baby with me when I went to the hospital to see my mother. The cancer treatment was having no effect and mum was starting to rely on pain killers to get through the days now.

The next morning we called as usual for Janet and her boys on our way to school. She said she'd give coffee a miss, if I didn't mind. She was making some new curtains and needed to get on with them. That's fine, I assured her, I was busy myself, what with the sitting room needing a coat of paint. We met up later that week on the way home from school. The children played together while we had a cup of tea.

A couple of weeks later I got a call from the hospital. I should go quickly, they said. I'd already picked up Alice from school and was feeding the baby. My husband, Dave, was at a meeting in Newcastle, at least three hours drive away. I phoned Janet. She would come right away, she said, her husband was already peeling potatoes for dinner at their house. Don't worry, she would see to the children and wait till Dave got home. I thanked her and called a taxi.

I phoned home around eleven. Dave answered. He assured me that Janet had fed the baby before she left. I told him they were giving mum another injection soon, a strong painkiller, they said.

"Go to bed, I don't know how much longer I'll be," I said, swallowing the lump in my throat.

It was around two in the morning when I got home. I put the kettle on for a cup of tea and poured a large brandy to go with it. I dabbed at my tears with kitchen roll, then allowed the warmth of the brandy to seep through my body and I was glad of the steadying effects.

I slid into bed and dozed a little, waking with the baby for his five o'clock feed. Dave slept on till the alarm went at seven-thirty, then came to put his arms around me in the kitchen. He seemed saddened by my grief. He promised to help me with arrangements, I was just to let him know what I wanted him to do.

I went upstairs, grateful for his care. I threw back the bed covers to air the bed, and a glint of gold caught my eye.

I picked it up, turned it between thumb and forefinger. The butterfly of an earring. My ears aren't pierced, I thought, neither are Dave's. Janet's are.

Ann Lloyd

What Do I Know?

I know that six times seven is forty-one,
That a Vicar's wife is called a Nun.
That Dickens wrote Domby and Daughter,
I haven't read it, but I ought to.

I know that baby sheep are Pups,
And Sussex hills are called the Ups.
That Tigers have spots and resemble dogs;
And sausages are made from Hogs.

I know that babies come from Hell.
And have a very distinctive smell:
That orange is a shade of blue,
And tapioca is made of glue

I know that Indians are born with feathers,
To keep them warm in colder weathers;
That all elephants have plastic trunks,
And happy donkeys sleep in bunks.

I know that water is made from ice,
And those tiny cats are called mice,
That blacksmiths work with coal,
And working men get the dole.

I know that Navy ships are painted red.
And in the end, when all is said,
You ask me what I know…

I'm still thinking about it.

I know nothing!

Clive Holliday

The Sound of Closing

The door marked Private closed for the last time on Tom Draycot. As every door has its own particular sound, so this one had a distinctive tone to its resisting ball-catch. Not that it had opened many times for Tom during his thirty-odd years at Machins Engineering. There had been no reason to traverse the area of expensive carpeting on the other side in all those years. Save for a reluctant request for a pay rise in the early days before the vast power of Unions took the necessity and caps out of workers hands. Then the constant whining of a disillusioned wife forced him to breathe the sacred air beyond that door. Now the vibration of the catch grated inside Tom's ears as he turned to walk back along the gloomy corridor. He glanced at his right hand, still feeling the pulpy wetness of the manager's handshake. He stroked the distaste down his faded dust coat, before stepping down onto the familiar concrete of the shop floor.

Redundant. The word spun round in his brain, spelling itself into senseless meaning. But he knew what it meant alright.

'Why me?' he thought. Harry Watson and Charlie Edson had already found the impersonal slip of paper in their wage packets, but they were younger men, hadn't his long service either.

Oh, his mates were sorry. Tom was a popular chap. They liked the careful, methodical machinist with his slow, thoughtful manner. If anyone had been rash enough to accuse him of meanness or violent action, they'd be laughed out of countenance.

'What? Old Tommy, theer, he'd let a mad dog bite 'im sooner than kick it int ribs.'

Somewhere in the shed a hooter sounded, ending the day shift. The last few men straggled through the swing doors beckoned by the prospect of home and family. Their laughter, no doubt at some ribald joke, echoed along the roof girders for a moment, then there was silence. The great pulsating heart of industry was stilled by the flick of a switch and only the generated hum of tethered power remained. Tom quietly moved foreward avoiding the sawdust crust of a grease spot. No spillage defiled his own massive Capstan. Its green paint smiled with pride at the bright steel curlicues of scrap beside an empty reject box. A few drops of cooling fluid oozed through the cutter's jaws and Tom automatically reached for a ball of cotton waste.

Again the resentment welled up in him. Anger pricked at the back of his mind to gain a stranglehold on his reserve. Tears smarted his eyes, blurring his vision. The sunlight which had found a metal rod to play with, spilled over into a hundred piercing splinters. A face swam before him, mouthing soundless words only memory could translate.

"Well, goodbye Mr. er – There will be severance pay, of course." Money! Who cares about money – it's a job I want. But she cares, the bitch. Want. Want.

"You're too soft, that's your trouble."

A cry like a wounded beast rose in his throat. His fingers slid along the bench till they touched and closed around the heavy length of steel. With repeated accuracy he brought it down on the undeserving lathe.

"Too soft, am I. Redundant, am I. I'll show you bastards I'm not done yet."

He staggered like a drunkard between the rows of drill gigs, turning his attention to anything within reach of his flailing arms, weilding the rod like a claymore with deadly results.

"Think you can throw me on the scrapheap, do you? Well, I'll make one for you – all of you."

The idea seemed to amuse him. He laughed a low gurgle swelling in volume, rising to a high pitch which the impassive walls bounced back.

They found Tom Draycot lying like a bundle of discarded rags in the devastation he had created. Silky trails of oil wormed along the uneven flooring, ending in a pool under his sodden boots.

A stray draught, seeking pleasure, caught a severed electric cable, lending it sensuous movement to caress an unwanted man.

Jo M. Hudman

The Porch

The times many they'd walked past the house and had never really noticed the new addition. The house was on the street that led to the junior school and many hundreds of big and little feet tramped, shuffled, hurried and lingered along the way. The cars raced past in their hurry to drop off their occupants. Not time to stand and stare.

"Well," said Mrs. Jones to her neighbour, "I can't say I've ever seen anyone to speak of, just occasionally the lights go on, but it's like a morgue." She gave a sigh at the thought of all that fat, juicy gossip gone to waste.

Her neighbour, Mrs. Peaches, checked up and down the road and said very quietly,

"People do say once you get inside that porch thing nobody comes out."

Mrs. Jones eyes widened and she quickly flipped the duster she was holding. It gave her something to do whilst she arranged her thoughts.

"Where did you get that from?" she asked, "if anyone should know it's me. I keep a close eye on this road and I've never seen so much as a postman walking up the front."

Mrs. Peaches took a step back, all her suspicions confirmed. Lots of the neighbours up and down the road had warned of the bitter tongue of Mrs. Jones so she had concocted this story and the bait was taken.

"Well, don't take my word as gospel, it could be that they work long hours," said Mrs. Peaches as she turned and walked back home, three doors down. Thank goodness I don't live next door, she thought, as she put the key in the door and was just about to step inside.

The sirens were loud as she shrugged her coat off and turned to put the kettle on. She'd just made the tea and was hunting for the chocolate biscuits she'd hidden when the front door bell sounded. She sighed and groaned, "What now?" as she made her way along the hall.

She opened her door to be met by several policemen, walkie-talkies all crackling a cacophony of noise so that she couldn't hear what was being asked of her.

"I'm sorry," she said, "what did you say?"

"Good morning, Madam, I wonder if you can help us? Earlier this morning we received a telephone call from one of your neighbours. The reported some carrying on at number twenty four. Have you heard anything?"

She looked at him in amazement.

"Well, how strange!" she commented. "We were only talking about it a few minutes ago, maybe half an hour."

The policeman immediately became more alert and started to ask more intense questions; "Who were you talking to? What did you say?" By this time they were in Mrs. Peaches kitchen. She'd made them a cup of tea and was waiting for them to drop at least a little hint of what this was all about.

"OK," the officer said, "here's what's happened. A body has been found in the back garden of number twenty four."

Mrs. Peaches was by now visibly shaken. The colour had drained from her.

"Who is it you've found?" she asked, hardly daring to hear the answer.

"We believe it's a neighbour," he replied, "who has yet to be identified. All I can say is she was holding a duster."

Valerie Holliday

Which the Vagrant

For just one moment out of a lifetime of moments
We shared a rusty seat
He so still, the emerald moss
Might creep from seeping wood
To gain admittance on his skin
And bleach the features free of tan.

Unkind sunlight picked at fraying cloth
Slid along a straining safety pin
Found its likeness in copper wire hair
Retreating when it reached the burning gaze
Defeated by the unfair contest there.

Owning nothing for possession's sake
No need of house for housing nothing
His misery a deeper thrill than
Cloistered virtue in a world of sin.

He knew I stared
As many stare who only comfort know
If eyes and lips were fashioned to disarm
Then he was master of the skill
And I forgot the hot sheep smell of wetted wool.

He spoke of many things denied to me
Truth, that knowing not
Make of minds a barren land
Planned for only bare necessity
He sought life's secrets, uncaring men deny
Who, caring less for purpose than for life,
reject the gift of reasoning.

I listened to his story,
Shaped by hands designed for giving not for gain
And I forgot the newsprint link
Of his last night's sheets.

I left him then, giving nothing
But having read,
Must now myself become the meaning
Not even turning to renew a memory,
That deadens at a second glance
Nor chance the odds that he was ever there.

For he was strange and sad and beautiful
And I forgot the word that folk will give
To such a man.

Jo M. Hudman

Prayers of Innocence

A PLAY IN ONE ACT

SCENE

(A dark prison. Mucky floor, stone walls. A high barred window. MAUD STAFFORD sits on an upturned bucket. She wears a dirty dress and shawl, and her face is dirty. Her hair, once tied up in an elegant style, now falls in disarray.)

MAUD

Is it Friday yet? Or only Thursday? They said I could see my Lydia on Friday, poor little mite. She's only twelve. She was scared to death in 'ere, she was. All the screaming and crying and shouting of godless words. I tried to cover her ears but what can you do when it goes on all day and night?

(pulls a crust of bread from her pocket and nibbles at it)

There's all sorts in here. Women drunk on gin and worse. Thieves and pickpockets. Gypsies and charlatans and fortune tellers. Respectable folk too, them's as fallen on hard times and 'ave accrued debts. Aye, and me, who never did nothing to nobody.

Poor little mite. She's not well. Three days it took em to drag us from Bakewell to Derby, then they threw us down here in the darkness wi'out even tellin' us what we was accused of. They took 'er off somewhere so she don't get infected by her mother's sin. Sin. That's a laugh, innit, what wi' me going to church every Sunday and Saint's day. She thought it were all her fault, see.

(She stands to pace, rubbing her lower abdomen)

I thought we were free o' this yesterday when the gaoler calls out me' name. We fair dashed up them stairs but we gets to the top and two men put shackles on us. 'You's off to see the magistrate' he says an I swear I never been so fritten in me life. We was dragged through passages and shoved into a courtroom what was full of learned gents in black 'ats an' gowns all talking and shouting. I was in a right state, up before all them men and me stinking o' the gaol.

I don't mind telling you I clasped me' ands and prayed to God that someone there would realise I was innocent.

MAUD (CONT'D)

Then the judge makes this funny noise an' everyone goes quiet. "Are you Mrs. Maud Stafford of the parish of Bakewell in the High Peaks?" he says, an' it all sounds so official I burst into tears. Well, 'e leans forward and tells me I been accused o' witchery and does I plead guilty or not guilty? O' course I told him I weren't no witch, just an 'onest working woman.

Then this other bloke stood up. Thin as a pole 'e was, like a skeleton covered in skin with a face like an 'atchet. I says to me'sen 'no good can come of a face like that.'

"My Lord," he says, and he 'olds up this sheet of paper, "I have here a sworn testimony that, on the night of the fifteenth of October, sixteen hundred an' eight, Mr John McTavish, an upstanding subject of the King, awoke in his room at the house of the accused."

I remember McTavish. I'll never forgive 'im for what 'e did.

The 'atchet faced bloke goes on. "He awoke because there was a strange light shining through the floorboards. He spied through the crack and saw Mrs Stafford and her accomplice, Lydia Stafford, engaged in suspect activities."

Well, what a bunch o' rot. I 'ad to smile. If that's what they'd dragged us here for they could bloomin' well drag us back again. Lyddie couldn't sleep, that's all. We was warming up some milk o'er the fire.

Anyway, the bloke looks at us an' back at the judge an' says "The culmination of these nefarious deeds was the accused declaring 'Over thick, over thin. Now devil to the cellar in Lunnun' whereupon they both did vanish and everything became as night again."

Well, the court went into an uproar wi' folk shoutin' an' yawpin and makin' such a racket as to wake the dead. The judge bangs 'is 'ammer until everyone quiets down again and 'atchet face goes on.

"So startled by what he had witnessed, Mr McTavish attempted to memorise the words, the better to tell the authorities. He realises now that it was somewhat foolish to repeat the words, for a great wind blew and transported him all tattered and torn in his nightshirt to a lamp lit cellar in London. There he observed the accused and her daughter bagging up parcels of stolen silks and muslins which they had obtained by witchcraft from the shops thereabouts. When she saw him, Mrs Stafford straight away passed him some wine in a bottle, which he drank and fell into a trance."

I shook me 'ead. What utter rot they was talkin'. Truth o' the matter was e was drunk and spun a petty tale that nobody would believe in a month of Sundays. I thought we'd be 'ome in time for Easter after that, but 'e just smiled a bit and carried on.

MAUD (CONT'D)

"Mr McTavish was woken by a watchman and taken before a magistrate on account of 'is suspicious circumstances. When His Worship enquired about his clothes, he said he supposed they were still with Mrs Stafford in Derbyshire, and when asked if he had walked to London in his nightshirt, he recounted the tale of being transported there by witchcraft."

And then, to make 'is point, 'e puts down 'is paper an' thumps the table with his fist, makin' all the court jump in fright an' says "Whereupon, My Lord, a warrant was issued for the arrest of the accused and her accomplice."

(gestures to her left)

I looked across at Lyddie an' she was all quiet, like. She'd been brought up to be bright and courteous up until I 'ad Mr McTavish to stay. It took me a week to coax 'er into revealing her troubles and then an 'ole night of 'olding 'er while she sobbed out 'er sorry tale, certain she was to blame and would be damned because of it. It was no wonder she 'adn't bin able to sleep.

Seems Mr McTavish, who was only ever upstanding afore the taverns opened, 'ad accosted my Lyddie an' promised 'er riches an' 'is 'and in marriage 'an then 'ad his wicked way with 'er an' told 'er she'd be damned for eternity if she ever told. It's no wonder she was bloomin' withdrawn, were it?

(shakes her head sadly)

Then the judge turns to me an' asks me if I've got 'owt to say in me' defence. Well I bobs a curtsey whilst I collects me thoughts. "Good Sir," I says. "I'm a God-fearing woman, barely scratchin' a living by makin' hats and providing lodgings. That Mr McTavish is a scoundrel, an' 'e forced his attentions on my poor girl an' when I discovered what 'e'd done I threw 'im out. I've kept his clothes and possessions, until such time as 'e pays me what 'e owes on his lodgings. That was more 'n a week ago, Sir. I ain't no witch, nor me daughter neither. We're good 'onest folk who go to church regular. I've prayed at the 'eadless cross in the churchyard every day since, pleading wi' God to take the sin from Lydia and give 'er the peace what is any child's right."

(slumps back to her bucket)

MAUD (CONT'D)

I would've swayed 'im, too, 'cept the 'atchet bloke says "I think we've heard enough, me Lord. The accused is clearly guilty, she even admits to praying at a headless cross and slanders the name of the very man accusing her. The prosecution rests." Then there's this fit o chucklin' through the court an' the judge bangs 'is 'ammer again and this other bloke puts a black 'ankie on the judge's 'ead.

"Mrs Maud Stafford," 'e says. "It is my sad duty to pass sentence upon you and your daughter. You have been judged guilty of witchcraft and will be taken from this court to a place of execution, where on Friday the thirty-first of October, sixteen hundred and eight you will be hanged from the neck until you are dead, and your bodies burned. May the Lord have mercy on your souls."

> (Light grows in the barred windows,
> where we see the outlines of two
> gallows.)

> (A long sigh)

An' that was when they took Lyddie away from me. I hope she's all right. Is it Thursday today, or Friday? They said I can see 'er again on Friday.

FADE TO BLACK

Absurd though it may now seem, this is the evidence upon which Mrs. Stafford and her accomplice were found guilty of witchcraft and executed at Derby in 1608. An unnamed Scotsman, who had had his clothes detained by Mrs. Stafford, went to London, stripped himself, and swore the above testimony.

My Home

Sitting outside first thing in the morning
A cup of tea my best friend of the day.
My eyes scan the garden, the colours are rich
I leap from my chair to check that you're there.

A walk into town just five minutes away
Hurry to finish the chores of the day.
The shoppers are flying from High Street to Market
Can't wait to get home away from it all.

Two wet noses pressed to the window
Patiently waiting ever since I left.
A voice calls, 'hello love, cup of tea?',
What more can you ask as you open the door.

This is the place for me to escape to
Familiar and warm, overflowing with books.
A mat that says 'Welcome', now that I'm back
I love the sound of my key in the door.

Valerie Holliday

Love on a Bridge

Salbris-de-Pont is a small quiet village in the Loire Valley. It has a cobbled square next to a bridge that straddles over a tributary that leads to the larger river a few kilometers away.

Gabrielle de Chambre was eighteen, pretty and curvaceous. She worked in the bank. The Banque de Paris closes its doors at midday and opens them again briefly at four in the afternoon. In the intervening period the people of the village take a small meal and a siesta.

At the moment that she had pulled the door and turned the key a young man asked in poor French if he was too late.

She recognised him as an Englishman immediately from the way he dressed and his accent. She replied in perfect English,

'I am so sorry,' she said, 'we open at four.' She paused as he looked crestfallen. There was something about him that touched her heart. 'Go and wait in the Cafe. Have a small meal.' She nodded towards the Petite Moulin Blanc. There were chairs under the awning of green and white stripes and a cluster of trees that provided shade.

'I am right out of Francs,' he said apologetically.

She took pity on him and opened her purse.

'Here, borrow these and come back at four.'

The exchange was witnessed by the cafe owner and he beckoned to the young man to sit. He brought him a beer and a baguette stuffed with spicy meats and tomatoes and placed a small dish of olives beside it.

'Our Gabrielle is a pretty girl, is she not?'

'Yes,' said Robert Davenport, 'very pretty.'

*****

A moment before the church of St Martin's clock struck four; Gabrielle came with her swinging jaunt across the square.

'Hello,' she called to the Englishman and passed him by to enter the Bank. An alarm briefly buzzed and then stopped. He followed her into the cool shade of the interior and came to the counter where she sat.

'Yes sir?' she said formally and gave a little smile. He passed his Traveler's cheque and asked for 3000 Francs. She read the name on the cheque and then smiled at him with the conclusion of business and closed her cashiers draw.

He hesitated at the counter and returned the currency note that she had given him earlier.

'I haven't paid for my meal at the cafe yet, and I was wondering if I may buy you dinner there tonight.'

She hesitated for just a moment.

'But yes. Meet me on the bridge at 8 o'clock.'

*****

Robert Davenport had suddenly fallen in love and he sighed wistfully. He stood on the bridge and threw a pebble into the stream. He had dreamed that one day he would find his true love. He now thought that he had. He was startled to hear St Martin's sound the bells of eight. There she was coming across the square. She was dressed in white and had a blue wrap across her shoulders, with a matching blue hand bag swinging at her hip.

'Good evening, Mr. Davenport,' she said with a smile, 'I thought you may have gone. But Voila! Here you are.'

She lent forward to receive a kiss on her cheek. Her perfume rose to engulf him in a stab of emotion. He trembled slightly as they walked to the cafe.

'My name is Robert,' he said.

'Oh yes. Ro-bair.' she paused, and repeated his name in the English style. 'Robert.' making an emphasis on the final T. 'I like that.'

They ate their meal leisurely, but Robert could hardly eat, his appetite had vanished as quickly as he had been struck by cupid's arrow. After the meal they stood on the bridge and they kissed. Tears of joy ran down his cheeks.

*****

Robert Davenport waited on the bridge at Salbris-de-Pont. Holding his hand was a young lady of just eighteen. She was dressed in white. The evening was warm and balmy. He picked up a small stone to throw in the water.

'Papa,' she whispered, 'Is this where you first kissed maman?'

'Mais oui, ma Cherie,' he said hoarsely.' C'est vrai.'

Clive Holliday

Black Widow

She waited motionless
Emotionless, blank,
Too still, her slender limbs,
Her eyes from his she drank.

He lingered fascinated,
Emasculated, spent,
Too soon the fatal kiss
Her lips to his she lent.

For him, no slow nerve-end decay,
No dark hole comfort in fly blown dregs,
No fear of weary palpitating heart
Or one times eight arthritic legs.

His life, the price of life,
For his like in perpetuity.

Jo M. Hudman

Helping Hands

One Friday morning Doreen grew perturbed. She'd always kept an open mind about the 'unknown' and 'supernatural'. Even watching 'Most Haunted' on the television didn't really frighten her. It was compelling viewing, intriguing perhaps, but quite unbelievable.

Now in broad daylight in her own sitting room, the ghost of a woman appeared.

Her days and nights of late and seemed so artificial. She couldn't even get interested in 'Coronation Street' anymore, a revelation in itself since the soap had always been her favourite, nor did the novels she loved to read, hold the same magic. In fact since coming out of hospital Doreen viewed most things with indifference. Was it the drugs she had been given making her feel this way?

What really hurt was the relationship with her husband; or lack of one. Barry simply ignored her; even the sparse conversations they once shared had become non existent. Doreen noticed how Barry had grown irritable; mooching around, shoulders slouched, and how when he thinks himself alone, he sits and broods, even weeps. Why couldn't he tell her what was wrong? It might allow her to understand.

For the last year their marriage had been floundering. Barry's redundancy at the engineering company where he had worked for thirty years had damaged his pride, his pocket too, since the government had messed around with pensions. Easier then to accept how he could reflect on the past…

…how he looked back when he left school and landed a job with its two year apprenticeship. He loved training as a draftsman, making new friends, learning new skills. They were given one day off a week to attend the local technical college, which continued into an evening course until 9pm. Afterwards they would meet since Doreen studied a secretarial course in the same building.

And then the redundancy. As if that wasn't bad enough it was followed by Doreen's hospitalisation. She assumed he would be overjoyed that the op' had been a success, that he'd be happy to have her home again. He could at least make an effort! She asked him if he had another woman, or, God forbid, had discovered he was seriously ill? The answer always silence.

Her being hospitalised over a month hadn't helped. Barry was hopeless at looking after himself. It had been their seventeenth wedding anniversary, the same day she was admitted to the hospital. He'd promised her a special night out at her favourite restaurant as soon as she was home and properly recovered.

Doreen had been home for a week, thankfully quite well and free of pain, yet still lacked the enthusiasm to do her Friday cleaning. Seated in her comfortable armchair in the living room she reached over to pick up a magazine from the rack. An involuntary shudder passed through her. The room felt chilly, her body numb, despite the coal fire Barry had made before going to work.

It was late October a time when her superstitious nature kicked in.

The magazine slipped from her hand to the carpeted floor, Doreen staring out of the bay window upon weather that did not look anymore cheerful she felt. A laden gunmetal sky reflected her mood. Heavy rain pummelled the leaded windows, trees devoid of leaves bent and swayed from their wind walloping. Gnarled branches reached out, Doreen convinced they intended to seize her. The poor woman hypnotised by the disquieting experience.

A draft passed around her legs, Doreen unable to believe it, when a woman in a grey dress covered by a floral overall, glided past her. Her sharp intake of breath registered her fear of the apparition; she wanted to run from the room, but was too mesmerised to move.

Open mouthed, she watched the thin elderly woman start to clean through the living room. Scarcely daring to breathe, Doreen stared with unblinking eyes, her dry mouth preventing her saying anything, merely watching as the woman enthusiastically cleaning then left the room.

Doreen sat up, trying to remain calm and to think it through. Has to be a ghost, she surmised. It's the only explanation. Perhaps she once lived here. That's it! We clean through on a Friday in case we have visitors at the weekend. Oh the poor soul, I must tell Barry.

Doreen never got the chance to tell Barry because he didn't come home that night; in fact he never came home all that week. Days blurred, became the same as any other day to her. Life seemed empty, she wondered from room to room searching for someone or something, though she couldn't remember what. Her frustration mounted.

Not a word from Barry. A letter arrived addressed to him that following Friday morning. Doreen spotted it on the mat but left it for him to pick up, whenever he chose to come home.

Sometime later, she noticed the letter had removed itself from the floor to the hall table, but how? There's only me in the house. It unnerved her. Making her way into the living room she recoiled, for there was the same old woman kneeling at their fireplace. Her head slowly angled to greet Doreen.

"My but it's chilly in here today love, I'd best make up this fire for your hubby, he'll need a warm house to come home to I'll bet.

Doreen couldn't believe this. Her fear increased.

"Oh please," she said, "go away. You're making me nervous. Just leave and don't come back again."

"I don't think so my love," said the woman. "Have you any idea where your husband has been all this week? He has been over to France to the place where you spent your honeymoon. If you remember you'll recall a family grave you so admired, especially the engraving on the headstone. You told him to remember it when your time came. He searched and found the photograph; unfortunately the inscriptions were not clear enough for the stone mason, so your feller took himself off for the week to see it again."

Anger surged within Doreen.

"Excuse me, but what has that got to do with you? And why didn't he tell me where he was going? Why on earth would he want to suddenly have a headstone made? It just doesn't make sense."

"My dear," said the woman, "I'm sorry to have to say this but it's time for you to move on, to leave this house and your husband in peace. Have you any idea what he's been going through lately? He is absolutely heartbroken, and cannot move on himself until you have."

"I beg your pardon! How dare you?" Replied Doreen. "You are the uninvited guest here, the one causing all our problems. Please just go!"

The woman gravely shook her head. "I'm so sorry my dear, you've got it all wrong. I'm obliged to come here every Friday to clean house for your widowed husband."

Ann Hodgson

Mining at your Fingertips

What of tomorrow
Or is it today!
Man power redundant
Robbed of his pay.

Mechanical mining
Geometry of face
Cantilever technology
Steps up the pace.

Automatic conveying
Power plants fill
Hydraulic robots
Controlled at will.

Then push-button mining
One man can feed
With rising population
More urgency of need.

White coat operators
Monitors of skill
Five finger exercises
Remote control can't kill.

Computed information
All will play a part
Fairy light patterns
Tap dancing on a chart.

Science fiction now a fact
You can take your pick
Nucleonic steer device
Or energy on tick

Jo M. Hudman

Shed a Tear for Scotland

How have I come to this miserable end? I am Mary, the sovereign Queen of Scotland. Once I was Queen of France too. I was married to that sweet François when I was just five years old. How old am I now?

I sometimes forget in the drab monotony of my imprisonment. Yes I was forty-four last December. And now tomorrow I am to be executed. I sit in this miserable place; Fotheringhay they call it. I call it the most desolate place on earth.

Well my little darling, you are now my only companion. What will happen to you tomorrow after I lose my head? I will ask one of the maids to look after you. You may be a small dog but you are my only true companion.

That jailor of mine, Paulet! God, what a miserable puritan he is. I am sure that when he gets to Saint Peter he will send him to purgatory so that he may be happy. The only time that I have seen him smile is when I kneel to pray. My joints are too weak now. He knows that I am in pain when I get on my knees.

Yes I have made a few mistakes. Why did I trust that boy Babbington? He was so charming. But I doubt that he knew that he was just a pawn in Walsingham's great chess game. But was he not just a servant to Elizabeth; that bastard daughter of King Henry. I should have been Queen of England, not her! Have I not the right of true succession?

The Lord is my shepherd; I shall not want.

Of course I want! I want to hold my baby! He will be twenty years old now. I had him as my child for less than one year. My darling James; and poor Darnley his father murdered. I have not seen the child since I was forced to abdicate.

What was the scheme? Babbington was to pass his letters to me hidden in a beer barrel that had a concealed bung. Then I would decode them and pass my letters out in the same fashion. That damnable man Walsingham was reading every letter and copying them. All those things that I had said about Elizabeth in my haste and anger; I did not really mean them; or did I? I get so confused. He was looking so smug at my trial. Like a cat watching a mouse. He was just playing with me. He was enjoying my discomfort.

He maketh me to lie down in green pasture: He leadeth me beside the still waters.

When was the last time I saw green pastures?

What day is it? It is the 7th of February. The nation will remember that I was assassinated on the 8th day of February in the cold year of, of? Damn! I can't remember. Yes it is the year of our lord 1587. That misery Paulet allows me so little warmth. I am so cold. It was February when I was sent to Tutbury Castle. And then I moved to Wingfield. I was happy there for a while. Elizabeth Talbot and I got on so well. We would sew together and laugh and play backgammon for hours on end. Then it was reported that I was happy. Well reasonably happy. Some spy reported me to my sister Queen. I was punished for being happy. Was that such a crime? Then there was all that gossip. It was suggested that I had taken George Talbot to my bedchamber and thus entertain him as if I were his wife. That redheaded cat Elizabeth Talbot treated me so coldly after that.

He restoreth my soul; He leadeth me in the paths of righteousness for his names sake.

I was only twenty-five years old when I came to this accursed country that should by all rights be mine!

Have I ruled this country for one moment? No I have been imprisoned. I have been left to rot in one stinking hole after another. What righteousness has there been for me!

Yea, though I walk through the valley of the shadow of death, I will fear no evil.

Evil! Elizabeth, she is evil yet I do not fear her. The shadow of death hangs over me like a macabre spectre. Why do I laugh? Paulet, he is the macabre spectre. I feel sorry for that man.

I will fear no evil, for thou art with me; thy rod and thy staff they comfort me.

Pope Sixtus will pray for my departed soul. And he will accurse that whore Elizabeth. She will pay a thousand fold for my miserable imprisonment.

Thou preparest a table before me in the presence of mine enemies;

Why should I have so many enemies? What have I done to deserve this?

Thou anointeth my head with oil; my cup runneth over.

What shall I wear tomorrow? Methinks that I will look best in my black gown with the lace collar. Or perhaps a white gown; no my blood will stain it. I will decide in the morning. I can't think about it now.

Buxton was pleasant. I enjoyed being there taking those waters. Five weeks I was there. It was so good. It was almost like being free again. But it didn't last, at the Shrewsbury's whim we went back to Chatsworth. Then we went to Sheffield. Then back to Buxton, then to Chatsworth again. I got quite giddy going back and forth with all my retinue that I had in those far off days. Now who have I got?

Surely goodness and mercy shall follow me all the days of my life; and I will dwell in the house of the Lord forever.

What goodness? What Mercy? I have seen so little of either.

God I ask that the executioner be swift.

And accurate!

And I will dwell in the house of the Lord for ever.

When I am gone will Scotland shed a tear for me?

And will I shed a tear for Scotland?

Where is that bloody priest?

Clive Holliday

In the Dark

It was not a busy day that day. Elsewhere in the library there was a hushed bustle and voices were subdued. In the reading room it was quiet, very peaceful. One or two of the regulars didn't appear to be here yet. Only the occasional shuffle of a chair, rustle of pages being turned and the odd, muffled cough disturbed the silence.

I had taken my usual seat and opened my book. The librarian had ordered it in especially for me and I couldn't wait to start reading it. Ah! the Colonel was close by, I could smell his aftershave. I had got used to him sitting at the end of my table. He only ever said good afternoon and goodbye, barking out the words as if he was issuing some sort of command.

I responded to his terse greeting as he pulled the chair out and sat down.

We had only been reading for about twenty minutes when the PA system crackled. One loud, piercing note shrilled. There was silence, total silence. No pages turned, no feet shuffled or throats were cleared. Then someone said, "The lights have gone out."

"You don't say," a gruff voice replied with more than a note of irony.

'So what?' I thought. To my surprise the book I was reading had proved to be very good and until now I had been enjoying it immensely. I didn't want anything to disturb me.

Tension filled the air, a sense of uncertainty surrounded me. Obviously people were rather concerned that the library lights had gone out. The silence had lasted for around half a minute when it was broken by the person who had stated the obvious and then there were coughs, sighs and whispering.

Feet suddenly shuffled quite close to me. A chair scraped across the tiled floor. There was a tinny bang followed by a deep male voice uttering the words "sod it." I presumed someone had walked into the filing cabinet to the right of me, perhaps trying to feel their way to the door.

I gripped my book, trying to keep my finger in it to mark my place. I wished these people would either hurry up and find the exit or sit down and wait for the lights to come back on.

"Hang on, I have a pen light!" a timid female voice echoed around the room.

"What good will that be?" the earlier, gruff, male voice resonated in the darkness. I was momentarily startled as he appeared to be standing close to me.

A somewhat huffy reply came, "It's better than nothing. Come on, shine it on the floor and we can follow the 'footsteps' to the exit."

There was a general hum of agreement and one or two chairs scraped across the floor as people began to stand up. Then there were a few more swear words as bags and tables got in the way.

"Try to follow the light," someone whispered, "you might miss the book cabinets that way." I'd noticed before that darkness tends to make people whisper. I could never understand why.

"It's probably a power cut, after all it is January and snowing outside." The owner of this comment seemed to be seeking confirmation of their statement.

"There should be a fire bell that goes off twice and then once again, but there hasn't been so it can't be a fire," a slightly shaky voice commented. As these words bounced around the room I tried to understand what everyone was so upset about.

Suddenly the table I was sitting at jolted and moved a little to the right. "Damn, that blooming well hurt." A peevish whining broke through the darkness. "Why can't they have round tables in these places and why haven't the emergency lights come on?"

I knew that voice. It belonged to the man who had been sitting at the end of my table. In my mind's eye I could see him, the epitome of a retired Colonel, always very abrupt but probably impeccably dressed with an air of authority which kept the library staff jumping to every little request he made.

Surely they had read the notices.

"The electricians have put the lights out of use," I said, surprised at the loudness of my words in the darkened room. For a few seconds no-one said a thing.

"Whatever, I will have something to say about it, you see if I don't," the Colonel responded loudly in the silence. "Why, may I ask, have they done that, leaving us all in the dark?"

Suddenly an excited female voice said, "I've found the door." It sounded like the lady who had the pen light, though she seemed more confident now. "Follow the beam of light and you will find me by the exit."

The lady with the 'lamp' immediately became everyone's heroine. Someone said, "Well done, my dear, yes, very well done."

There was a general hum and shuffling feet interspersed with the scrape of more chairs and more cries of "ouch, damn and bugger" as the table corners took their toll on the soft human tissue colliding with them.

I sat very still, waiting for silence to prevail and the lights to come back on so I could get on with my reading. I wondered why they all seemed surprised that the lights had gone out. The notice I had read was quite specific:

IMPORTANT NOTICE

THIS AFTERNOON AT 3PM THE LIBRARY LIGHTS
WILL BE TURNED OFF FOR NO LONGER THAN 5
MINUTES. THIS IS TO ENABLE ENGINEERS TO CARRY
OUT ESSENTIAL SAFETY TESTING

THERE WILL BE A WARNING BELL SOUNDED ONCE
ONLY IMMEDIATELY BEFORE THE LIGHTS GO OUT.

IF ANYONE DOES NOT WANT TO REMAIN IN THE
BUILDING PLEASE ENSURE YOU VACATE THE
LIBRARY

15 MINUTES BEFORE THE TEST BEGINS AT 3 PM.
THOSE REMAINING ARE REQUESTED TO STAY IN
THEIR SEATS UNTIL THE LIGHTS ARE TURNED BACK
ON.

EMERGENCY LIGHTING WILL AUTOMATICALLY
SWITCH ON IF THE TEST TAKES LONGER THAN 5
MINUTES

WE APOLOGISE FOR ANY INCONVENIENCE AND
THANK YOU FOR YOUR CO-OPERATION

A light suddenly switched on in my brain.

Was it possible my fellow readers had not seen the signs? Maybe they missed the notices. Most people seemed to walk straight past them without a second glance.

"Excuse me, did anyone read the notices saying the lights were being tested today and would go out briefly at three pm?" My question met with silence. Then someone said "What notices?"

"The ones in reception and I think in the lifts." My reply hung in the air like stale cigarette smoke.

Then a few annoyed and embarrassed murmurs slowly crept across the darkness of the room. It was at this point, as if by magic, the P A system burst into life. I felt several people, including myself, start in surprise at the announcement.

"We apologies for any inconvenience, Ladies and Gentlemen, the lights have now been tested and will remain on. We thank you for your patience and understanding."

I smiled to myself as I heard uneasy and annoyed mumbling, sensing that some people were embarrassed as they walked back to their recently vacated chairs or shuffled off in the direction of the lifts. Many of them intended to complain to the staff.

Feeling for my watch I thought, 'not bad,' it was four minutes past three, 'the engineers did quite well.' After all, closing the library would have caused a couple of hours disruption; treating everyone as sensible, intelligent human beings had surely been the best option.

Imagining the looks on the faces of my fellow readers, I smothered a giggle and returned to my book. Perhaps I should have mentioned I was the blind person whom everyone treated with so much delicacy and that the notice I read was in braille. Then again, for some silly, selfish reason, I quite enjoyed, just for once, having the advantage over my sighted companions that day, when the library lights went out.

Peggy Weeks

See You All Next Year

As soon as we felt the box move, we knew it was 'that time of year' again. Melissa, our Fairy Queen, was horror struck but I just sighed. Well, I've seen it so many times before and at my age nothing much bothers me anymore but I could hear the rest of the decorations muttering inside their newspaper wrappings. The date is exactly one week before Christmas, same as always. Time for the Klutz family to put up their festive tree and as we are the stars of the show our large, wooden box is being unceremoniously dragged down two flights of steep stairs. All around me is the sound of coughing and spluttering as my fellow decorations choke on fusty dust that gets shaken loose with every bump.

Perhaps I should introduce myself at this point; I'm Sid and I'm in charge of this motley company. I've been Head Snowman for quite a while now on account of I'm bigger than all the others *and* have lasted the longest. Heck, I've been around since Granny Klutz was a young 'un and that's a good few years! Suddenly, our battered box stops moving for a few blessed seconds. Could I be mistaken? Are they perhaps just moving house? No such luck! Within seconds small hands begin to tear at our box lid and those dreaded scrabbling sounds are followed by childish squeals of expectation.

"It gets worse each year," squawked Melissa as protective layers of tissue were ripped from her body, exposing her to the harsh lights of the Klutzes' living room and the gawks of its juvenile occupants. "Do they have no respect for royalty?"

"Quit moaning, Your Majesty!" I snapped. "At least you get wrapped in nice soft tissue when it's all over. All we get wrapped in is manky old newspaper that covers us all in ink, which then chokes us for the rest of the year."

I suppose I shouldn't have been quite so sharp with her but she really doesn't have a clue what it's like to spend most of your life covered in musty smelling ink that has to be rubbed off after we get unwrapped and usually by the not so gentle hands of the Klutz kids.

"Well, really," huffed Melissa, but she wisely left it at that and maintained a stately silence for the rest of the traditional unwrapping ceremony. As usual Tinsel and her all her stringy girlfriends have to be thrown away as they are squashed flat and have lost their shimmer but the family seem more prepared this year and I can see they've already bought replacements. Naturally Melissa, being Fairy Queen, can't resist a comment.

"If only the family bought quality this wouldn't happen," she sniffed. "I remember when tinsel was all fat and fluffy and sparkled for absolute years. It was gold, or silver, and a thing of beauty; something to be proud of and not at all like this cheap imported stuff in all colours of the rainbow."

"Quality lasts forever," she finally declared haughtily. "I mean; look at me."

"It's a good job that Melissa can't see herself these days," I whispered, rolling my eyes while the rest of them shook in soundless laughter. True, our Fairy Queen used to be a beauty in her day but that was a long time ago, way back in Grandma Klutz's childhood. Nowadays Melissa's pretty porcelain face is cracked, the regal robes of sapphire blue and silver are all faded and torn and she's even lost part of one wing but she still has her crown so we do allow her a certain amount of aristocratic leeway. Our Queen was at last installed, a little more roughly than she appreciated, at the very top of the tree where she will once more reign supreme for the entire joyful season.

Without much artistic grace the cheap lights from last year are now being draped on the plastic branches around us and, amazingly, all the electrics are working although for how long is anyone's guess. The junior snowmen have already got a pool going as to exactly how long before the first bulb goes. Meanwhile, the candy canes are predictably bitching about the heat from the lights.

"We always get put too close to the bulbs," whined Quentin. All the striped candy canes have their names written right through them just like sticks of rock at the seaside and they always insist upon being addressed properly.

"Balls!" said one of the original glass ornaments.

"I beg your pardon," said Quentin, turning sharply to see who had addressed him so crudely and spinning so fast that he went dizzy.

It was old Glasseye, one of the oldest surviving ornaments. "Glass balls like us get put close to the light bulbs all the time but we don't complain, not like you young 'uns."

"B-but you don't melt and go all sticky and misshapen," stuttered Quentin, "and you know that if we get too far out of shape we end up being eaten by those unpleasant children. We lost three good friends last year, you know!"

The poor old stick looked so alarmed that I took pity on him and whispered into his sticky pink ear.

"Just keep swinging when no-one's looking, Quentin lad, and you'll soon wriggle yourself far enough from the light bulbs to be safe."

When the Klutz family eventually retired for the night there was a little bit of restless shuffling and grumbling before the Tree, and all us decorations, finally settled down; resigned once more to our fate during the upcoming days of mayhem.

The week leading up to Christmas Day turned out to be not too bad though, all things considered. The eight–year old twins, Ray and Rita, had only managed to eat half of the chocolate soldiers between them but they did break three of the supposedly 'unbreakable' baubles, as well as several times knocking poor Melissa off of her royal perch at the top of our eight foot tree. The falling off however wasn't half as bad as the being hastily shoved back on again and by Christmas Day our poor Fairy Queen was a quivering wreck.

"I don't think I can take much more of this," she wailed after the last family member had staggered off to bed on Christmas Eve.

"Oh why couldn't they have given me to a charity shop last year after the sister-in-law said I was looking tatty? By now I might have been bought by some nice old pensioner who would treat me with the respect I deserve instead of having to put up with that little brat Ray looking up my dress every time he jams me back onto the top branch!"

Our Queen fanned herself vigorously with her one good wing while trying to ignore the hysterical laughter wafting up from the depths of the tree below.

"It's never been the same since we stopped having a real Christmas tree," I heard her mutter. Well, even if you're Royalty it doesn't do to complain too loudly these days you know; these artificial trees can be very nasty if they turn against you. But she is right. I've been around for a long time now and I can tell you that children used to be much more careful around the sharp needles of a traditional tree.

The morning of the 25th dawns to the shrieks and roars of the young twins as they rip into a mass of presents around the base of our tree: it must cost their parents a fortune each year. Chaos reigns as they race around showing off their new toys and knocking into our tree every time they run past. By ten o' clock their Dad, Arnie Klutz, has got well stuck into the lager, obviously intent on carrying on from where he left off last night. Grandma has also quietly uncorked the cream sherry and in between glasses is venturing to advise her daughter-in-law on how best to stuff the turkey. Such maternal advice has never been well received at the best of times but today it only adds to the rising gush of frustration that's threatening to overwhelm poor Dora Klutz.

Since last year our woman of the house has obviously become a little menopausal and is not responding well to such implied criticism of her efforts. By the time her younger sister arrives at midday, accompanied by a teenage daughter, a six year old genius son and their mangy dog it is glaringly obvious to all on the tree that Dora Klutz is rapidly nearing breaking point. Her successful, but divorced sister Daisy is 10 years younger but still wearing miniskirts and stilettos and she gives her older sibling an obligatory peck on the cheek before grabbing the nearest open wine bottle and draping herself around her brother-in-law's neck. Dora's blood pressure has now gone up another two points and it climbs still higher as the gravy boils over and yet, one way or another, dinner is miraculously ready in time for the Queen's speech on the telly. The Klutz clan duly gathers itself around an ancient, creaking, dining table.

Pru, Dora's sulky fourteen year-old niece wants to be anywhere but there at the table, as you would expect. She has refused to take out her I-Pod headphones to listen to the Queen's speech so the young twins are flicking sprouts at their cranky cousin across the table. Grandma keeps shouting, 'what did she say?' every time the Queen speaks so that nobody hears a word of the Royal discourse anyway. Glasses are raised, some more often than others, as a rapidly disappearing main course heralds the entrance of the old-fashioned British pudding.

Arnie Klutz has been watching re-runs of Masterchef lately: all a big secret from the family but of course we all know because we watch TV with him! Anyway, he suddenly has the bright idea of setting light to Dora's huge dessert in a suitably atmospheric room. I heard a faint moan of dread from Melissa up above but the rest of us just held our collective breath as, in the dimmed light, Arnie poured far too much cheap brandy over the rock-solid mound of Dora's efforts. When he touched a match to the pudding, blue flames shot five feet into the air, all the girls screamed and Granny's chair fell over backwards although the kids thought it was just part of the cabaret. Even the sulky teen-queen managed a smile, probably hoping that if the house burned down she could make a quick escape. Sadly, young Austin, her genius baby brother, knew exactly how to extinguish the flames safely so there was no need for the Fire Brigade after all and the family did eventually get to eat Dora's singed, seasonal creation. By that time, though, her blood pressure was well off the scale and she was past caring.

The excitement also proved far too much for the ten year-old mongrel pooch which ran around the living room in ever decreasing circles. I was so mesmerised that for once I failed to pick up on Melissa's squeaks of alarm as the animal gradually drifted in our direction. Suddenly it stopped spinning, cocked its back leg and peed like a racehorse all over our Christmas tree, then yelped as an almighty bang and flash of lightning plunged the entire house into mid-winter darkness. Order was eventually restored but not before Dora had accused her husband and sister of taking far too long in the cellar to fix the fuses An unpleasant row ensued and for the rest of the afternoon a fine veil of suspicion hung over the proceedings, in spite of much drink-induced merriment.

The dog later tried to make amends for his part in the seasonal chaos by systematically 'humping' any available leg, including all four legs of the dining table, until Arnie finally shut the uninhibited animal in the kitchen so they could all watch telly in peace. Well, relative peace considering Grandma's sporadic snoring. Shutting 'Fido' in the kitchen turned out to be a bad idea though when the Klutzes came to do the washing up and realised the dog had eaten the leftover turkey and stuffing!

By early evening the Klutz clan were all spruced up and off to the local Working Men's Club for the annual family party night leaving the tree, and all of us, in blissful peace. Well, except for the dog's stuffing-induced farting of course!

"Why on earth do they go through this ritual every year?" wailed our Fairy Queen. "My nerves are in tatters,"

"And I'm soaked in dog pee", wept Quentin, the dandy candy cane.

"Well, we've all got flash burns," screamed the not-so-glittery new Tinsel girls.

I sighed deeply, just grateful to have survived one more year without too many losses and so, forcing a seasonal smile onto my old grey face, I said "I guess that's it then folks!"

" See you all next year."

Katie King

A Mountain to Climb

Take my self,
Across a stream,
Quite a team

I carried a branch
Fallen, from a tree.
A stout piece
That I could see.

Casual clothes,
Good shoes

Silence in my heart.
Wonder in my stare,
As over trees I look

At last,
There it is,
Bright orange cave
I sit.
Only me,
My self

So silent
I am content

You made it then.
Silence to hear,
My welcome guest

Red robed,
No weight, nor dross.
Weightless silence,
A welcome guest

Elizabeth Procter

The Gloved Hand

It was New Years Eve, with snow still coming down, heavy and thick on the streets of Bradford. I set out to go to a friend's house for an evening party. I arrived at the bus station only to be told that no buses were operating that night. The taxis had the same idea.

"Sorry, love, no taxis tonight or tomorrow if they don't clear the roads."

I was beginning to wish I had worn my woollen dress and not my gold lame cocktail one. Fortunately I had the good sense to wear a warm coat

A young man also asked for a taxi, only to be told the same thing. We left the taxi office together. He asked where I was going and told me he knew the area well. As we walked up the road together he pointed out the short cut to the estate where my friend lived. I was a little shocked to see how very thin his arm was, and the narrowness of the finger that pointed the way, even beneath his woollen glove.

Of course it would mean walking through a wood alone in the dark. Studying the direction in which I had to walk it really didn't look too bad. I tilted back my head, face tingling as it caught the odd snow flake. The moon was full, the sky white with more snow. I felt no fear or trepidation only the excitement of the party to come. I turned back to thank the man and found him gone. I turned into the wood, the snow was light under my feet, not heavy, as on the streets. The only light I possessed was my mobile phone, boosted by the glow from the moon.

The eeriness of my surroundings together with complete silence made me slightly uneasy. Silly really, I was in the middle of nature itself what could hurt me? I had walked quite some way. From what the young man said it wasn't a massive wood, so I guessed I must be in the middle.

I stood perfectly still. I shuddered. With cold or just concerns with for safety I didn't know. My overactive imagination was beginning to take over. Being in what seemed to be the thickest part of the wood, the tall trees hid much of the moon. The light from my phone only allowed me to see my immediate path. I was about to move on, when a branch laden with snow broke away from its tree and landed at my feet. Its suddenness forced a scream. Roosting birds flapped and squawked so noisily it disturbed others on nearby trees.

Stepping over the branch I hurried on. The sound of a twig snapping took my breath for a moment; I stopped unable to carry on. Then light seemed to fill the woods once more yet I still couldn't move. A rustle from a nearby tree had me staring at its sturdy trunk. What developed I could not believe!

At first it was a mist which overlaid the trunk. Nowhere else, just on that particular tree. It undulated, rippled up and down the trunk; it grew thicker, moss green and grey colours emerging. I was a standing stone, staring at the apparition before me. In the moonlight, a beautiful young woman emerged from the tree. I watched, dumbfounded, as she stretched her arms above her head. Her star dusted dress shimmered as she stood; she looked around then hurried away without a backward glance.

I sat down much quicker than intended, I suppose it was the shock of it all. I banged my head on the tree behind me as I slumped.

Someone shook my shoulder. A brown knobbly hand with spindly fingers had roused me. I quickly jumped, needing to run to the end of the wood without stopping, intent on *never* entering a wood again.

I took a deep breath when the 'hand' pulled me back. I felt the tree trunk, cold, slimy and rough. I wrestled and tugged, the buttons on my coat were torn off, one by one.

"Please let me go." I cried, to no avail. I cannot remember a fear so terrifying as I was feeling at that moment.

"What do you want with me?" I dared to ask. To my horror I got a reply.

"My lady has gone, you are to replace her."

Once again I made to run but the 'hand' grabbed me. Fortunately only my coat was left in its clutches, my hand bag thrown amongst the rotting leaves. I ran, sadly not far, for in front of me I saw part of the massive roots of an oak tree, so I carefully jumped over each root knowing I mustn't fall, not now! The last one of the roots slowly lifted itself out of the ground. Surely my heart must stop. With the agility of a Boa Constrictor, it wrapped and squeezed its tendrils round my body; the hand wearing a woollen glove reached and clutched at my body and was puzzled as to why it wore a woollen glove…

The moon disappeared, leaving only darkness.

Ann Hodgson

There are noises at night

I know there are noises at night, creaks and knocks,
strange animal cries; there are shadows and spiders,
windows closed, doors locked,
when you're not here.

I know that geraniums won't flower for lack of water,
that moss grows wild in unmown lawns, pears strew
the ground, heaven for wasps,
when you're not here.

I know there's no need to shop for your daily loaf,
and skin-shrivelled apples overflow the bowl, bananas
grow soft, speckled brown,
when you're not here.

I know there are unloved corners in the garden,
bins full of compost wriggling with worms, undisturbed,
plants unstaked, unpruned,
when you're not here.

I know that milk lasts too long in the fridge and biscuits
go soggy in a tin and coffee dries in a jar, and the neighbours
don't call in for a cuppa,
when you're not here.

I know I'll not wake to the rattle of a tea tray with
the duvet,warm from the night, tucked tight, while rain batters
a reveille on the window,
now you're not here.

I know I'll never knit another jumper to lie beside
the folded ones in the drawer on your side of the bed,
your side, clean, smooth, cold,
now you're not here.

Ann Lloyd

Rebirth

Pete was shaving. It was an automatic process, freeing his mind to wander over matters both trivial and grave. Today, it was the comments of his workmates which flickered across his memory. . .

"What's the difference between snowmen & snow women? - snowballs!

The seven dwarves were having a bath & they were all feeling happy, but Happy got out of the bath so they all felt Grumpy!"

Immediately after the incident, they had all been concerned, sympathetic, even saddened by what had happened to him. But after a few weeks, he had recovered enough to start work again and in himself, Pete appeared to be more or less normal again as he carried out his duties as works electrician.

Then he began to notice, that mixed in with the usual behind the back comments about senior staff were other, more obtuse comments. Pete quickly realised that his mates were finding some amusement in his predicament.

Amongst nicknames like Fatty (Gibson, the overweight stores manager), Goofy (Snedden the toothy accounts clerk), and Sloping Shoulders (Smith, their laid back supervisor), were Whiteout, Blizzardy, Arctic and Bright. Jonesy, one of the lads who thought of himself as a repartee artiste, conjured up the expression Contra Black, which the others found hilarious.

Pete knew if he were to react, he would only become the butt of further hurtful comments, so he would briefly force a smile, and carry on with his work.

All these references stoked the images of the incident in Pete's head.

It was a six to two shift on a dark winter's Sunday morning. It had been a particularly good night at the club a few hours before. He had not slept well, and only for three hours. He was not, as they say, firing on all cylinders in the brain department. Questions like - why is the control box cover loose? Why has the heat shunt melted? And the all important - am I sure the power is off? remained unasked. The only question Pete was asking was - why did I drink so much last night?

Safety is supposed to be a priority in an electricity power station, but Sloping Shoulders had been at the club too. Little wonder he, too, was in no fit state to attend to his duties as health and safety officer. Pete and company had often pondered how on earth he kept his job – there had been many close shaves. They always concluded it was his glib tongue that enabled him to evade dismissal.

After 24 hours observation in the intensive care unit, Pete was sent to the burns unit for treatment. Whilst there, he was also visited by a trauma consultant, who encouraged him to discuss his feelings about his experience.

Lucky to have survived the high voltages that had slammed through his body, the main consequence had resulted in attracting all the hurtful wisecracks, for his hair had turned pure white!

Pete's razor finished its work. He had already eaten a cooked breakfast, washed up and tidied the kitchen. Putting the razor away, he thought about the day and the weekend ahead. It was a sunny Saturday in early May with an unusually warm light, southerly breeze. The week before, his instructor (whom he had not yet met) had said this kind of weather was ideal.

Pete's heart was beating a little more than normal. He had never contemplated doing anything like this before. Anticipation, nervousness and excitement melted together.

He had put his clothes for the weekend in the car the night before, together with crisps, mixed nuts, a few bars of fruit and nut chocolate, and a few cartons of Ribena. He was also taking his sleeping bag, for although the instructor had arranged bed and breakfast for him, he had no way of knowing how clean the place was, and he dreaded finding grubby bed sheets. Anyway, it was in his nature to leave little sign of his passing. Soon he was on the road, ahead of him a journey to the Lakes of some 3 hours.

Were it not for a chance meeting with a cousin of Sloping Shoulders, he would not now be taking this trip. A few weeks before, there had been a bit of an argument at the club about the difference between a canoe and a kayak. Cousin Sean, visiting from Norfolk, happened to know quite a bit about it, having spent more than a few weekends paddling on lakes, estuaries and canals. He proved to be an enthusiastic and knowledgeable advocate of the pastime. So enthusiastic, in fact, that Pete took him on one side to gain some uninterrupted information. Although he couldn't understand why, Pete was quite impressed, and some of Sean's enthusiasm got under his skin.

When Sean said he was attending a course in the Lakes, at Pooley Bridge, and invited Pete along, there ensued a question and answer session in which types of kayaks, equipment, safety gear, level of experience, etc. were all discussed. Pete was hooked. And never once did Sean make comment or even look at Pete's mop of pure white hair.!

So there it was, and here was Pete, heading for a beginner's kayaking course on Ullswater lake. Sean was booked on the advanced course, but they would be on the lake together, and most certainly would be in the pub later, discussing the day's happenings.

And that is just how it went. The weather stayed fine, the lake stayed smooth, the companionship and good humour were excellent. As sure as when

Pete's fiancé Aileen walked out for good and he felt a door slam shut on that particular romance, he felt a new door had opened just enough for the passion of a new found pastime to surge through and point him to new horizons.

A door he would never have known existed but for that chance meeting with Sean.

*****

Three months later, five weekend courses and one full weeks course under his belt, Pete felt not just a new, but a different man. Forward and reverse sweep strokes, draw stroke, sculling draw, stern and bow rudder, high and low brace. Pete could now perform these without thinking and could complete an Eskimo roll with breath to spare. He had already moved on to learning the reverse screw roll and was looking forward to when he could accomplish the hand roll, the roll without a paddle! Whilst he was still using craft from the training club's Pooley Bridge kayak fleet, he had already bought himself a neoprene wet suit and boots, cagoule top and buoyancy aid. His enthusiasm was such that he had also purchased a lightweight safety helmet, for when he had advanced to fast running rapids, with white water and spume covered boulders!

*****

He was, in essence, a different person. It was just nine months since his burns had healed but he had covered a lot of ground in more sense than one. Many times he had paddled from Pooley Bridge in the north, to Patterdale at the south end of Ullswater, a distance of some nine miles. Of course, he then had to paddle back, but usually with the benefit of the prevailing south westerly breeze at his back . He had often stopped on the way at the Ullswater sailing club, near to Watermillock marine park and had become quite friendly with some of the staff there. They had even suggested he might consider dinghy sailing and had offered a free introductory sail!

*****

It was now late August and since that painful accident the previous November, Pete had travelled far indeed. His confidence had grown almost with each paddle, as had his physical strength. He felt fitter in this outdoor environment. His mind took on a new dimension. He found he could now, for the first time, consider the sudden death of his mother, without shuddering. He really felt mentally far tougher, yet still retained the sensitivity he had been born with. The sensitivity that had been his Achilles' heel at work and which had been exploited by his shallower mates.

He had learned that in order to observe Ullswater's smaller inhabitants like water voles and shrews, he had to be patient, paddle very gently and keep a sharp lookout. Pete's increasing realisation of what nature had to offer in payment for his silent efforts served only to strengthen that sensitivity.

*****

Pete now had a plan. It had gradually come to him as the weeks and months past, gaining credibility over time, transforming from a possibility to a probability.

Loving Ullswater and the surrounding hills, he was already wondering how to spend more time there, when the senior kayak instructor mentioned there would be an instructor vacancy as one of the team was emigrating. Would Pete be interested?

Do apples fall to the ground? Does it get dark at night? Do slugs like lettuce?

Pete's plan instantly changed from probability to "definitely"!

A small chalet came rent free with the job, and although winters would be difficult- kayaking between December and April had little appeal to the punters, he had the house his mother had left him, which he could rent out, or live in himself. And he could always do some domestic electrical repair work for extra cash!

He felt the problems of the past peeling away. Aileen leaving – his mother's death - his workplace - the accident – being the butt of jokes. Peeling away like layers of an onion and in the middle, the very middle, was Pete the kayak instructor, Pete the smiling nature guide, Pete the sailor, Pete the new man.

The future had yet to build Pete the lover, the married man, the father. But all this would come to pass.

And Pete would always be an optimist now. His future family would love him for that alone.

Rarely now did anyone mention his pure white hair. And if they did, Pete didn't mind. He could take it now.

Keith Singleton

The Black Cat

I had walled the monster up within the tomb!

   The man eventually died, the cat bided its time.

   An age past, the house remained empty and fell into severe disrepair.

   The cat bided its time.

Edgar Allen Poe 'The Black Cat'

*****

"Emma, Emma! Come back here," the woman called, as the little girl jumped from the car and scampered towards the house, almost before the car had come to a halt.

Emma stopped. She hopped from foot-to-foot waiting for her mother. "Do hurry up, Mummy, I want to explore."

"Yes, but no dashing about. You know what the doctors said."

Emma sighed deeply; she'd been ill for as long as she could remember, some unspecified condition doctors hadn't got a name or cure for. She so hated being ill, and having to spend time in bed. She wanted to be the same as other children, playing in the street, running in the park. Oh, how she envied them.

Emma's shoulders drooped as she scuffed at a few fallen leaves.

"She's just excited, Wendy. Come on, Em, let's get inside," said Ray.

The cat stirred. Its waiting was almost over.

Ray unlocked the newly painted front door. Emma couldn't contain herself any longer. Despite what her mother had said, she ran from room-to-room up and down the stairs.

"I've picked my bedroom, Mummy. Come on, come on, I want to

show you now." With that she ran back upstairs.

Emma stood near the bed in the room she had chosen, stroking the satin bed covers. She skipped over towards the huge French doors, she turned the key and stepped out onto a large veranda.

"Be careful darling, don't get too close to the railings."

"Oh for goodness sake, Wendy, let the child enjoy her moment."

However Wendy's prediction came true when next morning Emma woke feverish and did not on her mother's insistence, get out of bed all day.

*****

The dawn chorus was in full voice and morning sunshine spread like a golden pool on Emma's bed. She stirred and sat up, she was feeling much better.

The cat stretched, it was time.

Emma heard a noise, she listened intently, her head tilted. That wasn't a bird, well not like any she'd heard before. There it was again. Emma slid from her bed, put her feet into fluffy slippers and went in search of the noise.

"Daddy, Daddy! Get up, get up, there's a cat in the wall downstairs," Emma shouted as she landed on her parent's bed pulling at the covers.

Ray sat upright trying to shake the sleep fog from his mind, he squinted across to the alarm clock, 5 o'clock it winked back at him, he groaned. "Go back to bed, Em, you've only been dreaming."

"But it is real, Daddy, I heard it. Hurry up! It will die if you don't hurry"

"Come on then," said Ray, knowing he wouldn't get any peace until he'd had a look.

"Wait for me," said Wendy throwing back the covers.

Emma wouldn't wait and ran off out of the bedroom and down the stairs.

Putting his ear to the wall where Emma indicated, he listened intently. There it was, at first a faint scratching then a mewing followed by a yowl.

"What are you doing, Ray?" Wendy asked, fastening the belt on her dressing gown and pushing her hair from her eyes.

"It's a cat! It must have happened when the workmen were here. God knows how long its' been trapped."

"Get it out, Daddy, plee-ase."

Ray fetched a large hammer and chisel and started making a hole in the cellar wall. Ten minutes later, a black cat covered in dust and cobwebs was extracted from its prison.

The cat shook clouds of dust from its fur and started to wash its face seeming none the worse for its incarceration.

"Can we keep it, Daddy, can we?" She pleaded, jumping up and down. "Please, please?"

"We'll see, we'll have to take it to the vet to check it over."

The vet gave the cat a clean bill of health and established it was a tom. The family returned home.

"We can't keep it, Ray, what about Emma?"

"We'll see how it goes. Emma's got no friends here. She's been uprooted and moved to this house, if it makes her happy we'll see, you must admit he is a very handsome creature, with his jet black fur and those intense yellow eyes. You never know it may be the best thing that's happened to her."

A large black shadow slid across the wall unnoticed by either of them.

When it was Emma's bedtime the cat took up a place beside her and curled up. Later when Ray looked in to see if everything was okay. Emma's arm was across the cat who looked up at him.

"It's all right, puss, I'm not going to disturb you." The cat blinked its huge yellow eyes and put his head back down.

As soon as Ray had closed the door he stretched and jumped down from the bed, he stalked across the floor to sit in the windowsill which was bathed in moonlight. He sat staring out of the window, waiting, waiting . . .

Julie Cawthorne

For KB

Something different has happened between us

I cannot place what, or when it befell

I know the aged well woven thread of our friendship

Has frayed and split apart.

Our tender years spent shaping each other

Our beginning, once fragile silk;

Adding strand by delicate strand

To strengthen and lengthen our bond.

How we fought to protect this thread!

Mutual battles, autonomous wars

Expanded the fibres of our alliance

We shared more than blood and bone.

Has this once thriving thread stretched beyond its length?

Or been torn by something unknown

I ponder the puzzle in sick, lonely hours

Through raw channels of fear

Which, when replaced with fiery anger

Rage through my veins.

Only in hours of grief for you

Do I allow the cruellest thought;

Perhaps you cut it

When I wasn't looking.

Kate Singleton

Purple Shoes I

Little Victoria tried to rub some life back into her cold chilblained feet. It was a long time since she had had the luxury of warm feet. She wandered the streets of Edwardian London running errands for farthings. She was saving to buy a pair of good leather boots. She had seen the fine ladies with their beautiful clothes and she thought little of them but at her low level she noticed the shoes peeping out from under the ladies long shirts. There was a stall in Whitechapel Road that sold second hand shoes. Ma Solomon specialised in other people's cast-offs. Victoria had seen the pair she liked. They were black with shiny buttons and a small heel. In the home that she shared with eight others she went to her hiding place and took her savings which now amounted to seven pence.

From her house in Stepney she walked the wet roads to the Whitechapel Road. Near the London Hospital she found Ma Solomon. The second-hand footwear stall smelt slightly. Victoria gazed at the jumble of shoes and finally saw the pair of black children's boots. She picked them up to examine them. Closer inspection showed them to be tattier than she remembered them. There were two buttons missing and the sole was nearly worn through. Ma Solomon saw her looking at the shoes.

"Try them on, my dear."

Although they were children's shoes they were a little big for her tiny feet, but she would grow into them and they could be padded out with some newspaper. Then she spied them, a most beautiful pair of purple shoes. They were small and dainty and feminine. She gasped and Ma Solomon caught the look of desire in her wide eyes.

"Not for you young lady, I want a shilling for them."

"I only have seven pence."

Victoria's spirits slumped and Ma Solomon shrugged

"You can have the black ones for thru-pence."

Victoria was struggling with her conscience. She knew that the black ones were more suitable but the woman within her desired the beautiful purple shoes to adorn her feet. This was observed by a passer-by whose heart was moved but this small female. She probably had never experienced footware in her life. There was a tinkle as a coin dropped to the floor. Mr Lehman stooped to pick up the shilling. He passed it to Victoria.

"You dropped this shilling young lady. You must be more careful with your purse."

Victoria accepted the shilling and with a smile of gratitude passed it to Ma Solomon.

"And I think that you can add the black shoes for another tu'pence Mrs Solomon."

Mr Lehman raised his hat and went on his way. The happiest little girl in London skipped all the way home.

Purple Shoes II

You could smell the war; a muddle of decaying flesh, cordite and raw earth. Men were doing their patriotic duty and dying in their millions. Young officers, incompetently trained, led their men to their death. Many more were wounded, their suppurating flesh delaying the inevitable burial party. The stations for the wounded lay a mile back from the front. Orderlies, tired and exhausted, did what they could to patch up these men. Many with minor wounds were repaired and sent back for another attempt at dying. There was a new batch of Voluntary

Aid Detachments or VADs. These women, who were trained in nursing and first aid, were barely ready to face the horrors of the hell that was to confront them. They were a contingent of sixteen from the East End of London. A bunch of lively women brought up on the hardship of surviving poverty, cheerful in any adversity. But this was not of their world. Their leader came into their billet. They had just arrived at a farmhouse serving as a field hospital. They were tired from the exertions of rough transport. No time to rest. They could hear the crup-crup of distant artillery.

"I want six of you in the stable yard to help with the new arrivals; quickly now!"

Amongst the six was a twenty two year old girl. She was slim of build with blond hair and blue eyes that were lively and intelligent. Her friend giggled nervously.

"Gaud help us Vikki, what have we let ourselves in for?"

"Well, Vi, we had better go and find out."

Their leader was a man who had served in the London hospital as a theatre assistant. He had been trained for the VADs and because of his previous experience put in charge.

"Set yourselves in pairs and attend to the new arrivals. Redress their wounds and make them comfortable. They may need washing and made ready for the surgeon. Victoria, I am putting you in charge of this consignment." He paused and gave them a smile. "Good luck to you all."

Horse drawn wagons and an occasional motorised transport brought the injured into the yard. Some were silent and some were screaming in pain. A priest went from man to man giving succour to those who needed it.

Victoria, accompanied by Violet went to her first patient. She smiled at him and instinctively took his hand while Violet sought his wounds. His leg was shattered below the knee. Victoria kept her smile although she felt sick. Violet realised that there was little to save and just covered the mess with a blanket. One of the other girls had run to the stable wall and vomited.

"The surgeon will be with you shortly," she said quietly, and they passed to the next patient.

"Hello and who are you?" she asked cheerfully.

"Private Lehman, 254," he said out of habit.

Suddenly Victoria was a little girl again proudly buying a pair of beautiful shoes from Ma Solomon in Whitechapel Road.

She lent over and kissed his forehead.

"Purple Shoes for a shilling," she whispered.

He lay staring at her.

"I remember," he said slowly and with a happy smile closed his eyes.

Clive Holliday

Common Form

If any question why we died.
Tell them, because our fathers lied.

Rudyard Kipling (1918)

A Dead Statesman

I could not dig; I dare not rob;
Therefore I lied to please the mob.
Now all my lies are proved untrue
And I must face the men I slew.
What tale shall serve me here among
Mine angry and defrauded young.

Rudyard Kipling (1924)

Swing Seat

"Hi, Gran, where do you want us to put these wrappings from the wood?"

"The cardboard goes in the green bin dear, the rest can go in the black bin. Now, you be careful with the seat she hasn't got a name yet."

Des and Bobby looked at each other and smiled. They had unpacked all the wood and

laid it on the ground.

"Well, this looks nice. Ouch! Watch what you're doing! I don't fit in there. Humans! Why can't they just read the instructions? All my wood fits in it's allotted place. Allotted, allotment. Oh, I made a joke! Alright, alright, it will sound better when I am assembled." Seat went into quiet respite, groaning only when the young lad tried to hammer in a screw instead of using a screw driver.

Des, the older grown-up, said, "Now, lad, lets have a look at them instructions. . . Then we can work

together better."

"Thanks, Gran."

She had set out drinks for Des and Bobby, her grandson.

"That's better," said Seat. "You will be fresh after a drink then we can get on. I want to view the garden properly."

Bobby and Des soon had Seat assembled and were lifting it into the holding frame, ready to clip it onto the chains.

"No, no!" cried Seat, "I will be too low."

Just then, her bottom landed un-ceremoniously on the concrete flooring.

"Ouch! What did I say?"

Des laughed, remarking, "Your Gran won't have far to reach." They both grinned.

Gran had not heard the remark as she watched from the conservatory and smiled. She was happy that they were getting on, because this was the men's first meeting.

Seat was now in place adjusted on her chains, to a reasonable height. Hands on hips, they stood back to admire their work, then nodded and walked away, happy, not hearing Seat speak.

"That feels like a good space behind me to swing. Privacy on my right and a nice plant area to my left."

Silence ensued as Seat swung gracefully. Bobby had given her a push as they left. She loved the space in front of her.

"I am going to like it here. Oh, hi," she called, as a fox glove bowed its head to her.

"My, you look good," he said.

"Hummm, take no notice of old Fox Glove. He's high and mighty at times." This came from a passing bumble bee.

A chorus of blue bells joined in. "You won't see us all the time, we only visit in spring."

"Oh! What's that around my leg," muttered Seat.

"It's only a cat," rippled Grass.

"Oh dear, cats leave a smell, so I was told by Grandfather Oak."

Bluebells nodded their heads tinkling in laughter. "Not this one, he's too old."

Cat purred against her leg.

"You've made a friend there," rumbled the knurled old apple tree.

Seat was silent in thought. 'What a lot to view and so many new friends.

It's different to the forest, but I like it here'. She shuddered as she remembered being taken from her roots, shaved, rolled and slapped by a human, just as he slid her into the saw blade. She'd had heard him say, 'this is a handsome piece of wood.'

"Best to forget all that," said the stately rhododendron.

"How did you know?" replied Seat.

"My ancestors were wild once, now we reside in parks and gardens. I even have a cousins living at a stately home. . ." Rhododendron paused for effect, which was lost on this new young thing, so he continued, "we live longer nowadays because we are looked after by humans. Fed in summer, composted in winter and trimmed come spring. We never dry out. Yes, it is a good life. Grandmother told us it would be all right in the end."

Just then seat was startled as a lady's bottom landing on her lap. They swung so easily together.

Gran smiled as she leaned back into the Seat, closed her eyes and gently ran a hand over seat.

"I like it. My Swing Seat," she sighed, her soft energy caressing Swing Seat.

Both content in nature.

Elizabeth Procter

Münchhausen By Proxy

Monday March 15th

Lucas was bad again yesterday. Pete caught him throwing stones at next door's Golden Retriever. The poor thing was chained in their back garden and couldn't get away from him. I think they'd gone out. When I asked him why he said the dog was an abomination and had to be stoned. Where does he even learn words like that? Honestly, I don't know what gets into him sometimes. It feels like he's the devil's own child.

I made an appointment to see his teacher after school tomorrow.

Tuesday March 16th

Mrs Handley was really kind. She'd wanted to talk to me about Lucas for a while but waited for parents' evening. She showed me some drawings he'd done. A man and a boy watching telly. Playing football. Holding sticks. Dancing. Sleeping. A man being shot by policemen and soldiers. She asked if Lucas had come into contact with any odd men. Perhaps an uncle showing more interest than was reasonable. I said no. The only men he comes into contact with are his father and his granddad. I asked her if I could have the pictures but she wouldn't let me. School policy, she said.

She couldn't shed any light on him throwing stones but asked me if he had any brothers or sisters. I told her he was an only child and she said he'd been bullying some of the other children. She asked if we were religious. I said we were C of E. She was pleased by that, I think. I didn't mention Pete and I didn't go to church, it's Pete's dad who takes Lucas every Sunday.

She wants him to see a child psychologist but when I said I couldn't afford it she told me I might be able to get it on the National Health if I see the doctor about it. I made an appointment for Thursday.

I asked Lucas about the drawings when I got home but he said they were something he'd seen on telly. Nothing to worry about after all. We shouldn't have put a telly in his room but I can't take it away now. I've told him he's not allowed to watch it after nine o'clock.

Thursday March 18th

Lucas wet the bed again last night. He'd been having funny dreams, he said, though he couldn't tell me what about. He wasn't upset. He played with his toy robots until it was time to go. Doctor Trent couldn't find anything wrong but did refer him to a child psychologist. I got Lucas to school just before the morning break and told Mrs Handley about the referral. She said it was for the best. Lucas has been bullying a lad called Ishmael. She looked at me a bit funny. I said we weren't racist but I could tell she didn't believe me.

Lucas seemed fine when I collected him at three. Happy as Larry.

Saturday March 20th

I've sent Lucas to bed without any supper. He is a horrid boy. Pete just laughed and told me it was perfectly natural for him to be curious but for heaven's sake! A dead cat! He swears he found it like that and I can only believe him but what sort of boy cuts up a dead cat when he finds one?

Monday March 30th

The psychologist was lovely, though I think she was too young to be a doctor. I suppose it's easier to relate to children when you're barely more than a child yourself. She talked to me first and I told her about the bullying and the drawings. I didn't mention the dead cat or the dead fox I found in his bottom drawer last week. I didn't want her to refuse to see him.

She sent me out of the room and talked to him for about twenty minutes. Afterwards she said he was suffering from 'religious mania' and suggested he stops going to church with his grandfather. She gave me a prescription for some pills he has to take twice a day.

Wednesday April 8th

Lucas broke the television in his room. That solves one problem anyway. We can't afford to replace it. Pete's had his overtime cut so we're barely making ends meet as it is. He'd done it deliberately, too. Said the voices told him to. I asked him what voices but he just shrugged. I get so cross when he does that. I'm glad we've got a follow up appointment with Doctor Jennings.

Friday April 10th

Doctor Jennings said Lucas was suffering from auditory hallucinations, probably as a side effect of the medicine. She put him on a different one but didn't offer to replace his TV the first lot made him break. She talked to him and he does actually seem to be getting better. Mrs Handley hasn't reported any more bullying and he hasn't done anything to animals for the last two weeks. Apart from the hallucinations I seem to have a normal boy again.

Sunday April 12th

I spoke too soon. Since he was getting better I let him go to church again with his granddad. At least I know what causes the episodes now. He came home with a sulk on, got changed and went out to play. He came home at five covered in blood. I dread to think of what he's done. I sent him for a bath and burned his clothes.

Monday April 13th

Mrs Jenkins has lost her cat. I didn't dare tell her Lucas had probably stoned it to death so I let her put up a poster in my window. Poor woman. She looks so upset. Of course, she hasn't got kids.

Tuesday April 14th

There's a missing kiddie on the telly. It's all over the news. Ishmael Choudhry from Lucas's school, missing since Sunday. I'm terrified. I know Lucas has done something. That was the day he came home covered in blood. He swears he doesn't know what happened to the boy but I found his tablets stuffed down the side of the armchair in the front room. He's been spitting them out. He said sorry but I couldn't get an ounce of sense out of him through the tears. I sent him to bed without his tea.

Wednesday April 15th

Still no news about the missing kid. The police have assumed foul play. There were pictures on the news of them doing searches in a long line. Mrs Jenkins's cat turned up. Lucas hadn't done anything to it after all. Her old man locked it in the tool shed by accident.

Thursday April 16th

They found little Ishmael stuffed into a suitcase and dumped only three streets away. Someone called the council about the smell and there was this little kid all cut into pieces up inside. Nothing to do with Lucas after all. I'm so relieved. I don't know where the blood came from if it wasn't the cat or the kid. I'm just glad it's all over.

Monday April 20th

Doctor Jennings spent forty minutes with Lucas and said she was 'concerned'. What does that even mean? I told her he was better but she said she'd have to refer him to another specialist, one that looks at people's brains. I was terrified again. Had Lucas got a tumour? We had to go straight to the hospital by ambulance and they X-rayed him and put him in this big metal scanner. It took the whole day but afterwards they said he was all right and sent us home again. What a waste of time! These doctors don't know what they're doing half the time.

Friday April 24th

Mrs Handley called me into the office when I went to collect Lucas. He's started bullying again. I don't know what I'm going to do with him. 'You don't know what bullying is' I said. I'll teach him right from wrong if it's the last thing I do.

Monday April 27th

Took Lucas' to see Doctor Trent again. He had these weird marks on his hands and feet. Stigmata, the doctor said, though Lucas isn't Catholic. Probably self inflicted. The doc thinks he's being bullied. What am I going to do?

Tuesday April 28th

Lucas was ill again last night. He threw up everywhere so I kept him off school. Pete's dad looked after him. We're really busy at work and with Pete's reduced hours I can't afford the time off. It's probably one of those twenty-four hour things.

Wednesday April 29th

Lucas still off school. Poor lad. We've put our telly in there for him. Pete's dad is helping him with his reading, too.

Monday May 4th

The school phoned about Lucas being off. They need a doctor's note for him as it's been a week. First I've heard of sick notes for kids but apparently it's a new government regulation to cut down on truancy. Makes sense, I suppose. Lucas is no better. He just lies there. He didn't even want his dinner yesterday. Pete's dad has gone down with it as well. We put the spare bed in Lucas's room. It makes sense to keep them together. They keep each other company while I'm at work.

Tuesday May 5th

Pete and I had a row tonight. He went to look in on Lucas and his dad and came out looking sick. I asked him what was wrong and he pointed back to the room and shouted at me. Told me I was a stupid cow. He can talk. Lazy sod he is. I'm holding down a job and looking after his old man as well as Lucas. He never lifts a finger around the house. He stormed off and I watched telly until the early hours.

Wednesday May 6th

Pete didn't come back last night. I phoned his work and they hadn't seen him either. I've a good mind to change the locks.

Thursday May 7th

Mrs Handley dropped in today to see how Lucas was. She asked for the sick note but I forgot to get one. She said it would be fine if I got it tomorrow. She left me a bunch of flowers and a card they'd made in class. All the children had signed it and written little messages. It was really sweet. I took it in to Lucas but he didn't care. I think he's soiled the bed again. That's the second time today. I swear he's getting worse. I'm sure he does it to annoy me.

Friday May 8th

Pete's dead! I feel awful now. They found him in the woods between here and the pub. They think he was jumped on the way back the night we had an argument. His wallet was gone, which is why it took them so long to identify him. Blunt force trauma, they said, but I know that means his head had been bashed in. I watch the crime programmes. Now I've got a funeral to arrange on top of everything else. I won't tell Lucas just yet. I'll wait until he's better.

Saturday May 9th

I applied for a funeral grant from the victim's compensation scheme and put in a claim for Pete's life assurance. It's amazing what you can do on the computer these days. I asked Lucas to help but he couldn't sit up for more than a minute or two.

Monday May 11th

Two police officers came today. They'd had a complaint about the smell. They were ever so nice about it. Apologetic, even. I explained about Lucas and his granddad being ill and I was looking after them. The lady officer was quite sympathetic. She was a mum as well, I could tell. They suggested I call a doctor in if it was that bad and would I like a visit from the community worker to see if they could offer any suggestions? I thanked them but said no. No need for people to be poking their noses in.

Wednesday May 13th

Different policemen came yesterday with a warrant to search the house. Two of them went upstairs and one of them was sick all over the landing. I warned them Lucas was infectious but would they listen? Now I've got that to clean up. They called for an ambulance and took Lucas and Pete's dad away but they wouldn't let me see them. They put me in a police car and I've been at the police station ever since. They took my fingerprints and put me in a cell as if I was a criminal or something! Then they showed me stuff they'd taken from Lucas's room. A hammer and a knife and a saw, all covered in blood. What's he done now?

Thursday May 14th

More questions. They showed me two suitcases and asked if I recognised them. Of course I did. They were mine. The vanity case and the little case. I told them I used to have a big one to match but someone pinched it. I told them they should go after wrong-doers like them as did Pete in. Not innocent mums like me or kids like our Lucas.

I had to ask for paper to write my diary on and they'd only give me a pencil. It's downright criminal, the way they treat folk.

Friday May 15th

They've put me in a different place now. It's a bit like a prison and a bit like a hospital. They make everyone take drugs to keep them placid. I only pretend to take mine. I'm keeping my diary to let people know what really goes on. I've done nothing wrong and they treat me like a loony. They still won't let me see Lucas.

Monday May 18th

Pete's funeral today. They let me go to it though they handcuffed me to this woman in a uniform. I think they were scared I'd make a scene about them not looking for the thugs who killed him. There were two other funerals, too, and I had to wait through all of them before I could leave. They are round the bend. They won't let me see Lucas but they make me go to some stranger's funeral? What's up with that?

Friday May 21st

They won't let me see anyone. They keep me locked in this room and I'm not allowed any visitors except for an endless succession of doctors and policemen asking me about hammers and Pete's head and his dad's head and the bruises on Lucas. How should I know? They won't let me see anyone. What bruises, anyway? If they've hurt my Lucas I'll swing for them.

Why won"t they let me see my boy? They can't stop me seeing him. I'm his mum. He needs me.

Rachel Green

Picking Daisies

"William?" Melanie started.

"Hmmm?" William's concentration was on the oil level on the dipstick he was wiping clean on an oily rag. Melanie's nose wrinkled at the rag – where did William come by them? He had an endless supply of colourless, shapeless scraps.

"William!" she snapped.

Sensitive as he was to any change in an engine's tone, William recognised the crisis in Melanie's voice. Now that she had his attention, Melanie took a breath.

"Do you love me?"

"Hmmhh?" William was taken aback.

"Do you love me, William?"

William studied the dipstick again, then slid it back into the oil sump.

"What's brought this on?"

Melanie ducked her shoulders out of reach as his greasy hands started towards her.

"Well, I was doing the daisy thing in the park and all I kept getting was 'loves me not,' so I want to know. Do you love me?" William studied the seriousness in Melanie's face. For once, she wasn't smiling, her lips had no colour. Her skin glowed from the sun in the park, but her eyes were dewy.

"Well, I wouldn't be with you if I didn't, would I?" William hedged.

Melanie considered the last couple of years. It had been fun, mostly, and they cared about each other, helped each other out. William looked after her car, she washed his football kit. He cooked dinner once a week, she filled in his tax returns. Friday nights in The Crown with mutual friends – was that it? All or nothing she'd decided in the park.

"Only, usually after a couple of years or so, most people feel they want to be together all the time. Do you feel like that, William?"

"Well, we do spend most of our free time together, pretty much, don't we?" he mumbled.

Melanie's tone deepened.

"So, let me see how this works. You don't love me enough to tell me that you do love me, and you think we already spend enough time together."

"Well, I don't think I'd put it quite like that," William said, "anyway, I really must get this service finished..." and his head went back under the bonnet.

"Yes. Okay, William, you get on. I've held you up long enough."

Checking the spark plugs, William didn't look up as he spoke.

"I'll pick up the usual from the Golden Sun on my way over tonight, shall I?"

Melanie was already getting into the driver's seat of her car.

"Don't bother," she said, sliding the key into the ignition, "I think I could do with a change!"

Ann Lloyd

A Means to an End

Act 1
Scene 1

Scene : A public square in Some Town
Enter: A Market Hall

He speaks...

Oh, what discontent o'er shadowed all seasons
And all the clouds that lower'd upon my stones
My bruised face used for doleful meetings
With dreadful marches in bannered measures
To wage grim visag'd war on my wrinkled front
And caper nimbly in a council's chambers.

But I, that am not shaped to court a looking glass,
I, that am rudely stamp'd for want of majesty
Curtailed of fair proportion
Cheated of former feature by my crown's dissembling,
Must I be sent before my time
Into some unbreathing world, scarce half remembered
Am I so lamely and unfashionable
That only dogs delight in dog high structure
And rats take pleasure to gnaw my bones.

With no delight to pass away the time
Nor spy my shadow in the sun
I, therefore, since I cannot prove an asset
Am determined now, an eyesore so to prove
And blame the cursed men who made me thus.

Plots have been laid and suggestion dangerous
By drunken prophecies, plans and schemes
To set those who are for me and those not so
In deadly hate, the one against the other.

But, if these Cestrefeldians be as true and just
As I am ugly, false and treacherous,
This day should see agendas neatly sewed up
About a prophecy which says that, I , my own murderer shall be
Dive thoughts, down to my soul,
Here the bulldozer comes.

Exit

Jo M. Hudman

With apologies to William Shakespeare

A Knock at the Door

Rose stood at the kitchen window just gazing, watching the birds flying from tree to tree. They were frantically seeking insects to feed their new chicks, occasionally visiting the feeders hanging from the trees. Suddenly as one they all swooped and flew off. I wonder what's disturbed them. She looked round the garden thinking to see a cat, but no, nothing. Her peace was disturbed by the doorbell. Ah good it must be the postman she hoped.

As she opened the door she stepped back in amazement. The young woman smiled, "I'm sorry to trouble you, I wonder if you can help me?"

Facing Rose was the strangest looking young woman. Her first thought was to close the door, then her sense of doing the right thing took over and she forced a smile nervously. Facing her, the young woman looked like an alien; she was dressed in black from head to toe. The only colour she wore was a bright purple-black lipstick and the longest dangly earrings made up of every colour of purple. Rose lost count of the studs and piercings lining her ears. A thought flashed through her mind as she summed her up. If she got rid of that black hair dye and had a proper hair cut, she could look really pretty. The girl was watching Rose's reaction, not at all put out, this was quite normal so she waited patiently. "I'm so sorry how can I help?"

"My name is Mattie Custer and I've just moved here to attend the university. Originally my family came from here then moved to Essex where we all grew up. I've been tracing my family roots and I think we are connected somehow. I wondered could I talk to you about it, I can call back any time convenient to you or meet someplace. It would be great to get this piece of the puzzle sorted."

Rose by this time had counted a dozen studs along the edge of one ear and numerous sleepers, as well as the danglies and was totally absorbed in the task. Mattie stood quietly waiting. Suddenly Rose realised she'd stopped talking and was looking at her in amusement.

"My dear, I'm so sorry, will you come in, I'll put the kettle on and you can give me the details, if I can answer your questions no problems." Mattie stepped inside and was just about to undo the laces on her boots when Rose said, "Don't worry love, by the time you've got all the laces undone it'll be time to put them back on, I can see they're clean enough". Mattie smiled and thanked her. Rose was busy putting the kettle on and arranging the tea tray.

"Tell me Mattie, what part of Essex were you raised in?"

"We lived in a little village that backed onto Epping Forest, we had a wonderful time growing up and the forest was our backyard so to speak. We camped in it during the school holidays; all my brothers and sisters loved it too, so we made quite a crowd when our friends joined us." Rose smiled, "I used to enjoy camping too; the freedom is quite delicious, just to come and go as you please, to cook or get a takeaway. Mind you when we used to camp the only takeaway was the local fish and chip shop".

"How many siblings have you got?" Rose poured the tea and pushed the cup towards Mattie. "Thank you, all together I have five brothers and three sisters, mum says nine's her lucky number so we can all relax." She laughed at Rose's face and shrugged, we used to joke and say mum was going for a football team and they could be called 'Custer's Last Stand', but dad said enough, any more and he'd take to the garden shed. Rose was amazed at the confidence and utterly relaxed manner of this girl. "How old are you Mattie?"

"I'm the eldest and I have just had my twenty fifth birthday."

"What are you studying at University?"

"Human genetics, I'm just working on my Doctorate so shouldn't be too long before I'm out in the big wide world paying off my overdraft. I've been so lucky, especially with my tutors; they've all really supported me and pushed me in the right direction."

Rose was totally out of her depth by now, the lass facing her and the story she she'd just heard didn't Tally. She'd seen these youngsters who dressed in a non-conformist way, but never associated them with having a brain. "I bet your parents are really proud of you aren't they?"

Mattie smiled and reached for her handbag.

"It's really kind of you to give me your time, I have a picture here of the family I'd love you to see." She produced a folder selected a picture and passed it to Rose.

"Just a minute love, I'd better get my glasses."

Rose sat back down and picked up the photo. There was a deathly hush before Rose could speak; she gazed at Mattie. "I don't understand."

"It wasn't until you opened the door that I finally did. I can't believe it, but it must be true, you are the double of Mum." She sorted through the folder and handed Rose a Birth Certificate. "Will you check that against your own?" she asked.

Rose stood and quickly left the kitchen making for the sitting room. She found it and hurried back. By this time her hands were shaking. They compared dates, hospitals, parents, everything tallied. Rose was feeling surreal and kept thinking to herself, I'll wake up in a moment it's all a dream.

"How come you've managed to find me Mattie? It's like the last piece of the jigsaw finally fitting. For years I've felt incomplete is the only way to describe my feelings, as though something was missing." She sat back in her chair her face awash with tears.

"I do understand," said Mattie, "mum always said she felt as though something was missing from her life, but could never put her finger on anything specific. It wasn't until I started to trace the family tree that things didn't quiet add up."

"What sort of things do you mean?" asked Rose, as she wiped her eyes.

"Well, when I checked on the census two babies were named, a Rose and Belinda. Rose was noted as the eldest and of course Belinda is my mum. So we were really curious by this time and I managed to trace you through that, although you had disappeared as a baby, it was almost as though you didn't survive, but nothing proved otherwise."

"Honestly Rose," Mattie sighed. "It's been a real roller-coaster and mum is so excited she hardly dares hope its true. You know all the lost years and what could have been; it's endless really isn't it?"

Rose just sat, she was stunned, and she couldn't get her thoughts together. Mattie got up and sat closer to Rose, she put her hand on hers.

"Rose I'm so sorry, I can tell it's been a shock, would you like me to go, maybe we can we can meet and chat some more when you've had time to digest it all".

The tears were rolling down Rose's face again. She looked at Mattie."Do you realise what this means? You could be my niece, and to answer your question, no I don't want you to go, please stay I have so much to tell you, but I need to sort it out in my head first. She squeezed Mattie's hand. Let's have another cup of tea and some lunch and you can tell me all about your work, it sounds fascinating."

After they'd had lunch and cleared away Mattie said, "Now's the moment I can't put off any longer, Mum will be dancing an Irish jig wondering how I've got on, do you mind if I give her a ring and pass on the great news?"

Rose looked at her thoughtfully. "I think it's about time love, don't you?"

Mattie got her phone out of her bag and pressed the buttons, they were both waiting on tenterhooks as it rang out. After the second ring a faint voice was heard to say "Mattie, is that you love, tell me quickly?"

Mattie had a big smile on her face on her face, all she said was. "Bingo mum". She handed the phone to Rose.

Shyly Rose took it and said,"Hello Billie, it's been such a long time."

Valerie Holliday

If I Had Never Dreamed

Last night I thought I had a dream. This morning I turned my brain inside out looking for that dream but couldn't find it anywhere and then I began to wonder - what would life be like if I had never, ever, dreamed at all?

If I had never dreamed then I could never have sensed the freedom of unfettered flight. Once, while talking to my sweetheart in my dreams, I watched in amazement as his beloved face softly melted and he transformed into a giant butterfly which then winged high into the air with me, somehow, safely aboard its delicate back. We soared and dipped and fluttered through a magical garden, gently pausing now and then to allow him to sip at the rich nectar of a thousand rainbow-coloured blossoms. We were soon joined by other butterflies of all shapes and sizes until the air all around was a fizzing cauldron of colour, bubbling away under the warmth of a summer sun. On and on we sailed, forming a colossal cloud of delicate wings that flickered and flecked in the afternoon brightness. Eventually my painted chariot tired and he fluttered down to rest, ever so gently, on the warm sandstone of a low garden wall. As he rested there awhile I proudly watched my lover sunning his wings and showing off his brilliant markings. In the way of dreams he was first a Red Admiral and then became a Purple Emperor, proudly wearing his rich colours as they vibrated and pulsed in the warm sunlight. All too soon he set off again, fluttering and dipping as butterflies do but always climbing ever higher until he finally disappeared from my view.

Saddened by his departure I set off alone to continue my dream on foot, wandering away through a cool, green glen and along the banks of a small stream as it danced down the valley. Its waters sparkled as they tumbled over moss-covered stones, reminiscent of jewels spread upon a velvet cushion; perhaps a starry-eyed offering from my still absent lover. A vast canopy of midsummer trees, pierced by the sharper angles of stark evergreens, gave shade to my weary body as I strolled. My bare feet were cushioned by a soft carpet of fallen leaves and pine needles and forgiving moss that squished coolly between my toes.

Then in an instant that cool and calming citadel vanished and my bewildered eyes were drawn upward in awe at mighty mountain ranges that towered over me. In the rapidly gathering dusk I then became a bird of prey, soaring up a looming cliff face and out into the rosy hues of a sunset-filled sky. I was a majestic eagle, or maybe a modest hawk, or perhaps even an owl - I could not say which – but I knew for certain I had become a bringer of death on silent wings. I flew higher and higher into that glowing twilight until I hovered over some small, unsuspecting creature going about its nightly business below and then I pounced. Proudly, I carried off my prize and headed home to feed supper to my helpless young; perfectly designed avian hunters who would, in the fullness of time, grow to become as skilled as me. I suddenly realised that the cycle of dream life would continue long after I had moved on. It would be as if I had never even been there and the thought somehow disturbed me, even though my dream journey continued.

If I had never dreamed I could never have been absorbed into the beauty of swimming beneath ocean waves. The open sky was left far above me as now I easily, effortlessly, glided through those deep, crystal waters; vast oceans that churned with the living motion of hundreds of fishy friends circling around me, with all of us turning and swerving and darting as one. I moved within that aquatic ballet as though born to marine life and my once clumsy land-limbs flowed elegantly in serene slow-motion as I passed unrestricted through vibrant coral reefs and shadowy caves, totally at home in a whimsical, watery world.

Sometimes the crusty carcasses of dead ships would magically appear out of the ocean's disconsolate depths, revealing their secrets and treasures. Once-proud Spanish galleons rested forlornly among the sleek silhouettes of modern Cruise liners and as I slowly drifted through those nautical skeletons I was mesmerised by their sad reminders of lost lives. Everyday items from steerage passengers were strewn around the seabed like discarded toys and even the squirreled-away possessions of long-dead aristocrats had managed to escape from bondage. I stared in astonishment at case upon case of gold coins and fabulous trinkets; tantalising treasures whose earthly beauty had remained untarnished by their decades of submersion and which now offered luxury homes to humble shellfish.

Later I found myself drifting through the ugly consequences of human conflict; among turrets and keels of slaughtered warships that scarred the seabed and whose thunderous weapons of death were now forever silenced. These vessels were from many Navies and some were even from ancient, once vibrant cultures but all were once manned by similar men, with similar families, who had all suffered the same awful fate. My tears of compassion were well meant but they too would drown in those salty wastelands and my sorrow would go un-noticed by the ocean's living, but cold-blooded, inhabitants.

If I had never dreamed I could never have tasted the acid fear of being lost and alone. On dry land once again, I wandered among abandoned buildings and found myself shuffling through a maze of endless corridors and empty rooms; scary, solitary spaces that constantly unfolded, one into the other, and yet led me nowhere. I seemed doomed to ramble in ceaseless circles, always returning to the same vaguely recognisable room no matter what door I chose to leave by; a room that seemed both familiar and yet terrifyingly harmful to me, like a favourite slipper might hide a scorpion lurking within its soft lining. At other times I would struggle through swathes of spider webbing as I battled ever onward, stumbling toward the light that I could always see but never quite reach. I gasped and fought as if life was being squeezed out of me by some invisible foe until it felt as if my very will to survive was being tested: as if I were being mockingly asked – 'are you ready to move over to this side yet?' – and I sensed that if I should hesitate with my answer I would be doomed. The light of eternal hope was always shining just ahead of me, if only I could reach the end of the next dark and dangerous passageway.

Then those endless rooms gave way to a dark urban landscape and the sense of urgency grew even stronger in me. I ran breathless and alone through a warren of bleak and rain-soaked streets; always hearing someone, or something, rushing up behind me and set on doing me terrible harm. I could taste the harsh bile of dread rising up in my throat at the sheer terror of having nowhere to go, nowhere to run to, and no escape from such unseen and unknown malice.

At last I awoke; in a sour cold sweat and gasping and panting with panic yet experiencing an overwhelming tsunami of relief as I realised that I was still alive!

If I had never dreamed then surely I would never have really lived at all, for without the ability to dream can a person truly *feel* anything?

Katie King

Sadie's Revenge

Amy Pemberton had lived at Riverside Cottage for twenty years, the last eight of them alone, except for her cat Sadie. Her husband, Fred, had inconsiderately pitched head first into one of his prize rose bushes he'd been deadheading one Sunday morning. He had died instantly of a heart attack.

To give him his due, though, he had left her very well provided for, quite rich actually.

Amy loved the cottage situated as it was by the side of the river, close to the boatyard and Marina.

She could sit in her garden watching the river's passing seasons. From the bright blue summer days, to grey snow-laden winter skies. In summer, she would watch the people enjoying a day's boating. Rowers from the local rowing club sculled up and down. Happy people called out cheerily to Amy as she sat under the cool trees on her lawn in the heat of summer.

In the quite time of the year she saw the river's wildlife, the ducks diving head down, webbed feet in the air, the shy water voles entering the river with an almost silent plop and the herons standing sentry, ever alert for a silver darting fish to catch.

Amy was quite content with her life as it was, strolling around her garden tending to the flowerbeds, accompanied by Sadie, her cat.

There was just one cloud on the horizon: her nephew, Stanley, as her only living relative. He'd taken to visiting often since the death of his uncle, knowing he would inherit everything when Amy had gone.

Amy didn't like him. Never had. He put her in mind of a squat pink toad with his thin wet lips over which his tongue kept flicking nervously, his pale bulging eyes which darted to-and-fro, missing nothing. She remembered Stanley as a child, not very fondly. He was indulged by

Amy's sister who had spoiled him rotten. He was materialistic always wanting the latest everything.

As if thinking about Stanley had conjured him up, there he was ambling down the garden path large as life and twice as ugly, for all the world as if he already owned the place.

He was his usual ingratiating self, fawning and sucking up to her, pretending to care and only to have her best interests at heart.

He'd brought some smoked salmon for her tea, fresh strawberries and a bottle of wine for them to share.

Because it was such a warm day they ate in the garden.

Amy enjoyed her tea, tempting Sadie with tit-bits of salmon. Stanley curled his lip in disgust at the cat being fed at the table, especially with the expensive salmon he'd paid for. No there was no love lost between the cat and Stanley.

Amy wondered how long it would be before he started on his favourite subject. Sure enough, after enquiring about her health and what she'd been doing all week.

"Well, Auntie, have you thought any more about selling up to the boatyard owner? He won't keep the offer open forever you know."

Mr Stannard, the Mariana owner, had wanted for some time to buy her house and land so that he could expand his business, but Amy had always rejected them.

Amy was a small, neat little woman with iron-grey hair and she had an iron will to match, more than able to stand up for herself against Stanley.

Replying crossly Amy said, "I never would, and never will sell out, your uncle Fred would spin in his box if I did! I won't sell while I still have breath in my body."

Amy stood to go indoors, picking up Sadie who had been asleep on her lap. Sadie gave a parting venomous hiss at Stanley over Amy's shoulder.

"Maybe that can be arranged," Stanley muttered.

Later that night after her nephew had left, Amy made herself a cup of hot chocolate, chose a book to read, and retired to bed. She began to relax from the stress of her nephew's visit as the hot drink and the warm bed worked their magic. With Sadie asleep at her feet, all was well once more.

Amy woke with a start, and looked at the illuminated face of the clock. Two a.m.

What was that noise? Was there someone in the cottage? Her heart thudding as she got out of bed, Amy made her way onto the landing, calling out.

"Who...who's there?" No answer. Starting towards the stairs Amy suddenly felt an almighty shove in her back, then nothing.

As she lay twisted and broken at the foot of the stairs, Stanley stepped out of the shadows on the landing, smiling to himself. He had been waiting there since sneaking back into the cottage.

When he switched on the light, Sadie was watching him from the top of the wardrobe, with a flash of her green eyes and swish of her tail. She'd seen what he had done.

Stanley went downstairs, locked the cottage door and slipped quietly away. Of course he had to feign shock and sorrow when the police told him of his aunt's 'accident'.

Stanley was staying at the cottage for a few days to clear things out and finalise its sale to Mr Stannard.

But things hadn't gone quite as Stanley had hoped. His aunt must be made of steel. She had survived the fall, even though he could have sworn that life had been extinct. She might even have succumbed to the cold, lying there on the floor all night, if it hadn't been for that dammed cat sitting on her giving her just enough warmth to stay alive.

Talking about Sadie she was always there on the edge of Stanley's vision, staring accusingly at him, but she was never close enough to catch.

Still, things weren't all bad, Stanley had got power of attorney as his aunt had been in a coma for several days after her fall. Long enough for him to put the sale of Riverside Cottage in motion and rub his hands at the price.

It was almost certain that his aunt would not return, and what good was the cottage to someone in a nursing home? When he could spend the money from the proceeds and enjoy himself. On the last night of his stay and with everything settled, Stanley congratulated himself on being so clever. Since Mr Stannard was due to exchange contracts tomorrow, Stanley celebrated in style with a thick juicy steak and all the trimmings for his supper, an excellent bottle of wine followed by several glasses of Brandy.

Making his way none too steadily up to bed, he didn't see Sadie as she wove between his legs on the top stair.

Julie Cawthorne

Epitaph.

The best thing I can hope for

As the Lord turns out my light

Is to hear my children's friends say

"your dad was a bit of a prat - -

but he was alright- - - -

- - - All right"

Keith Singleton

About Quirky Quills

We are a group of writers who meet every Monday at Chesterfield Library from 2 to 4pm. We formed in June 2009 and have built a membership of keen writers of all genres. Tutors and speakers occasionally come to generate enthusiasm and interest. We feel we learn from each other's strengths and skills and work together in a vibrant and enthusiastic team to improve our writing.

In 2010 we published our first anthology. We sold 300 copies and all profits were were used to provide art equipment for the Nightingale Childrens' Ward at the Royal Hospital, Chesterfield.

The profits from Fragments will benefit Ashgate Hospice, a local charity well known and loved in this area. Ashgate has been very supportive and we are pleased to be partners in this venture.

We have an open door policy and although we do not consider ourselves to be a teaching group, we welcome new members whatever their background and experience. If you have some poems, short stories or a few chapters of a book tucked in a box at the back of a cupboard, you would be welcome to come along and share some of it with us.

You can contact us by email:

quirkyquills2012@gmail.com

We are listed on the Derbyshire Arts website, and are on their e-mailing list.

Further copies of our Anthology can be obtained from your local bookshop, online via Amazon or by contacting us directly.

writing

is a bit like walking

in that you put one word after another

until you reach the end

(which this is)